ALL-IN

PETE HAUTMAN

New York London Toronto Sydney New Delhi

SIMON & SCHUSTER BFYR

An imprint of Simon & Schuster Children's Publishing Division

1230 Avenue of the Americas, New York, New York 10020

SIMON & SCHUSTER BFYR is a trademark of Simon & Schuster, Inc.

For information about special discounts for bulk purchases, please contact Simon & Schuster Special Sales at 1-866-506-1949 or business@simonandschuster.com.

The Simon & Schuster Speakers Bureau can bring authors to your live event. For more information or to book an event, contact the Simon & Schuster Speakers Bureau at 1-866-248-3049 or visit our website at www.simonspeakers.com.

Also available in a SIMON & SCHUSTER BFYR hardcover edition

Book design by Steve Kennedy

The text for this book is set in Melior.

Manufactured in the United States of America

First SIMON & SCHUSTER BFYR paperback edition February 2012

10 9 8 7 6 5 4 3 2 1

The Library of Congress has cataloged the hardcover edition as follows:

Hautman, Pete. 1952–

All-in / Pete Hautman.

1st ed.

181 p. ; 22 cm..

Summary: Having won thousands of dollars playing high-stakes poker in Las Vegas, seventeen-year-old Denn Doyle hits a losing streak after falling in love with a young casino card dealer named Cattie Hart.

ISBN 978-1-4169-1325-2 (hc)

[1. Poker—Fiction. 2. Gambling—Fiction. 3. Poker—Juvenile fiction. 4. Science Gambling—Juvenile fiction. 5. Las Vegas (Nev.)—Fiction. 6. Las Vegas (Nev.)—Juvenile Fiction.] I. Title.

PZ7.H2887 Al 2007

[Fic] 20

2006023871

ISBN 978-1-4424-3335-9 (pbk)

ISBN 978-1-4424-3336-6 (eBook)

Acknowledgments

Thank you to K. J. Erickson, Ellen Hart, Mary Logue, Bill Smith, and Deborah Woodworth for help with the story, to Jim Hautman for vetting the poker scenes, and to David Gale for waiting.

ALL-IN

1

(Jimbo)

THE KID WAS TALLER THAN AVERAGE, MAYBE six-three, but you didn't notice it so much when he was sitting at the table. Mostly what you saw was that shock of dark hair like somebody took an egg-beater to it, and sunglasses so small and dark and close on his eyes they looked like black holes in his head.

He usually wore a track suit, black with blue stripes. No tattoos, no watch, no rings, no nothing except for a necklace of gold beads that looked more like something a girl would wear. I asked him about that once, but he just gave me this look like, *Dude, don't go there.*

Most figured him to be twenty-five, twenty-six. Going on forty. But I knew Denn Doyle's real age, which was technically not old enough to vote, join the army, get married, or play no-limit Texas holdem at the Sand Dunes, which is what he was doing the night I saw him go broke to a pair of black aces.

A guy like me sees a lot of poker hands in a lifetime. After the first hundred thousand deals it's like you seen them all. I've had four kings get beat by a runner-runner draw to a straight flush. I've seen more sets of trips cracked than most people have hairs on their heads. I've seen a man bet his last hundred dollars on a 44-to-one shot and hit it, and I've seen him take his winnings and do the exact same thing the very next hand.

But until that night I never saw a guy bet twenty grand on the stone cold unbeatable nuts and lose it all. Because in theory it just don't happen that way. The best hand is supposed to win. That's what the game's about, the way it's always been.

You know how Texas holdem works, right? You get two cards facedown and you bet 'em. Then the dealer lays out three cards faceup in the middle of the table—what's called "the flop"—and you bet again. Then he puts a fourth card on the table—"the turn"—and you bet again. The fifth and final board card is called "the river." One more round of betting, then you show your cards. Best five cards—

using the two in your hand and the five on the board—wins. Easiest game in the world.

I'm at the Sand Dunes playing holdem, $75-$150 limit, when I hear that Bill Frisk and Morty Deasel are hot to play some no-limit, $5000 buy-in, $25-$50 blinds. Me, I like a big game, and I think I can beat these donks, so I say I'll sit in and play three-handed for a bit, see what develops. I was thinking maybe we could get a tourist to sit down and take a shot at us.

Yousef, the cardroom manager, sets us up at a table up front next to the rail, and we play for a while.

A half hour later, Denn shows up with those little black glasses he wears. He eases into the three seat between me and Morty and pulls out a rubber-banded roll of hundreds and counts it down. Sixteen thousand dollars.

The kid maybe used to be loaded, but I heard he'd been running bad lately. Real bad. I heard he dropped ninety large in one night at the Bellagio. And something about the way he counts off that last hundred tells me it's his case Franklin—his last hundred-dollar bill. He loses that, he's tapioca.

I notice Denn isn't wearing his gold necklace. Wonder if he hocked it.

Morty and Frisk eye him like two hyenas trailing a wounded wildebeest. Morty pulls out his roll and

buys in another 5K, and so does Frisk. They don't
want to be short-stacked. Never mind the kid's rep
as one of the most dangerous holdem players in
Vegas—the hyenas smell blood.

Del the Cabby, who still drives a taxi even
though he's about eighty years old, sees all the
money hitting the table and wanders over to check
out our action. He watches us play a few hands,
then sits down next to Frisk.

"Buy-in's five, Del," says Frisk.

With a wrinkled, veiny hand, Del pulls out a roll
big enough to choke an alligator. Del the Cabby isn't
just a cabby. He owns half the cabs in Vegas.

Now there are five of us. Me and Denn Doyle and
Morty Deasel and Del the Cabby and Bill Frisk. And
for a while it goes bet, raise, fold. Bet, raise, reraise,
fold. Bet, fold. Playing no-limit holdem is like being
in the marines—hours of boredom punctuated by
moments of sheer terror.

After about an hour, the kid is up a couple thousand. He's playing good, picking up more than his
share of blinds, being aggressive but not stupid. One
hand he raises it up $500 preflop. Del the Cabby
scratches his lumpy nose, then shoves in his entire
stack.

"Call that bet, kid," he says.

The kid thinks for about a minute, his face

showing absolutely nothing. "I can't call," he says, throwing his cards away faceup. A pair of queens.

"No balls," Morty said. "Pocket ladies, I'd have been all over that one, kid."

Del the Cabby shrugs and shows his pocket aces with a sour smile.

Everybody laughs. Morty laughs loudest.

Like I said, the kid was playing good.

Frisk and Morty are both screwed down lug-nut tight, playing only big pairs. I should've smelled a rat right there, on account of Morty is usually a pretty loosey-goosey-type player. I must be getting old.

I should probably introduce myself, even though you maybe heard of me. My name is James Robert Cowles, but everybody calls me Jimbo. I play poker for a living. I been making it at this game for four years, two years in Tunica and two in Vegas. I play mostly tournaments. I got two World Series of Poker bracelets, and I made the final table at last year's World Poker Tour. You maybe seen me on TV. I'm the guy with the long hair and the bowler hat.

I see a lot of younger players coming up the ranks lately. A lot of them online kids, not very talented, but there's always a few get lucky. Most of them, by the time they get to be my age, will have got broke more than once. That's when you find out if you've got what it takes. Get broke and come back a few times. I've done it. I'll probably do it again. I mean, I might look like an old pro to a lot of these newbies, but the fact is, I'm all of twenty-two, Stu.

Denn Doyle was the exception that proves the rule, or so I thought at the time. As far as I knew, he'd never once been broke. Last summer he'd destroyed some huge game back in the Midwest and actually won himself a restaurant off some high roller. But he was only sixteen, and no Donald Trump. After just a few months he ran the joint into the ground, converted his remaining assets to cash money, and headed for Vegas. You got to be twenty-one to play here, but fake IDs are easy to get, and the kid has a face on him you can't put an age to. A few months back he just showed up at the Bellagio, sat right down in a $400-$800 game, and destroyed it.

I met him a few days after he hit town, and we got to be friends. He fascinated me. Like I say, he was a kid, just turned seventeen, but if you looked at the way he played, the way he carried himself, the way he bet his chips, you'd say he'd been gambling for a thousand years.

But back to this game I was telling you about. We been playing for an hour or so with no really big pots. The kid has a little over $19,000. I got $6400. Del has made a couple of bad moves and is down to $2500. Frisk and Morty are sitting on maybe twelve grand each. Morty—some guys call him Morty the Mouth—has been trash-talking, giving Denn a bunch of crap.

"I hear those boys at the Bellagio been giving you some chump lessons, kid."

Denn ignores him.

"Guess they figured they'd fattened you up enough. Glad they left some for me."

The kid pulls out his iPod and plugs in. He doesn't want to listen to Morty no more, and I don't blame him.

And then we get into it, the thing I'm telling you about.

It starts when a new dealer sits down, this redhead named Cattie Hart, and I see the kid's face go soft and slack, like somebody slipped him a roofie.

I know the kid is having a little thing with Cattie; they hooked up a couple weeks back. I can't blame him—Cattie is pure fox, right down to the red hair, the clear brown eyes, and the canine smile. But Cattie does not so much as give the kid a look. She is all business, her smooth face hard and tight, shuffling the cards with professional speed and precision. Like Denn, it's tough to put an age on her. But however old she is, the cards flow like butter in her hands.

Morty bets $500 out of the small blind. Frisk, in the big blind, instantly calls him. The flop comes ace, deuce, jack. They both check. The turn is another jack. Check; check. The river brings a ten. Morty makes an oversize bet of $8000. This is a strange thing for Morty to do, but he does it anyway. Frisk calls and shows a king, ten. Morty shrugs and folds without showing his cards.

I've seen a lot of fishy plays in my time, but that was one of the fishiest. It looked as if Morty had just given Frisk an $8000 gift. I didn't get the point of it at first, but it didn't take long for all to become clear.

Three hands later I wake up with a pair of jacks in the big blind. I like pocket jacks. Some guys say they're the toughest pair to play in no-limit holdem, but I like 'em. Lots of guys like to raise with 'em, but not me. I like to get in cheap, then catch a good flop or get the hell out.

The action goes like this: The kid, under the gun, limps in, calling my blind bet. Morty also calls. Frisk raises it up to $600. I do not like him raising that way after both the kid and Morty limp in. Limpers are dangerous in no-limit holdem.

Del the Cabby folds. I look at my jacks and get this creepy feeling running up my spine. Maybe I have the best hand. Maybe not. Regretfully, I pitch them into the muck.

The kid calls Frisk's bet. Morty picks up his cards and stares at them. Very sloppy. Holdem players usually leave their two hole cards face-down on the table and just lift the corners a little bit to see what they've got. Morty actually lifted his cards up off the table. I can see that he has a nine of clubs in his hand, and if I can see it, so can the kid. Clearly, Morty is going to fold. But I am think-ing that it is very uncool of him to flash his cards that way. I'm surprised when Frisk doesn't raise an objection.

Morty mucks his cards. Cattie raps the table, burns the top card, and flops an ace, king, nine. The kid stares at the flop for a few seconds, then checks. Frisk bets $1000, a small bet given the size of the pot. The kid calls. At this point I read the kid for a monster—pocket kings or pocket aces.

The turn card is another nine. The kid checks. Frisk bets $4000. The kid smooth calls.

The dealer peels off the river card. A third nine. Interesting.

The kid stares at that nine for about twenty sec-onds; then he checks. Did he smell a rat? Or was he slow-playing? One of these days I got to ask him.

Frisk pushes forward his entire stack, about

$15,000, enough to put the kid all-in with his last $14,000.

The kid frowns at his cards. He must have a sixth sense or something. He unplugs himself from his iPod and looks at Cattie. She doesn't look at him. He stares at her for a long time, then he shrugs, turns up his pocket aces and says, "I call."

His hand is unbeatable. With ace, king, nine, nine, nine on the board, the best possible hand would be four nines. But I saw Morty fold the nine of clubs. The kid saw it too. So his aces-over-nines full house has got to be the stone cold nuts.

Frisk, squinting at the kid's pocket aces, shakes his head slowly, as if he can't believe he's lost. Then he turns up a king. I think he probably has another one, giving him kings over nines full. But the second card he shows us is the impossible nine of clubs.

I expect the kid to jump up and start screaming. I mean, that's what I would do. But he just turns dead white and stares at that card for what seems like forever but is probably only ten seconds, and then his head comes up slowly and he looks at Cattie.

She is staring down at the table, blank as a slack-strung marionette.

Frisk has this little smile on his face; Morty is inspecting his fingernails.

Del the Cabby shakes his head slowly.

"Tough beat, kid," he says.

Denn shoots a look at Del; then he looks back at Cattie.

"Why?" he says to her.

Cattie says nothing.

Yousef, sensing a situation developing, comes bustling over to the table.

Denn, his voice brittle as ash, says to him, "Look at the tape." Meaning the video recording from the hidden cameras that dot the cardroom ceiling.

"Is there a problem here?" Yousef, struggling to get up to speed.

Color is coming back into Denn's face, red rising up from his neck. He shoves his chair back, stands up, and thrusts a finger at Cattie. "She set me up," he says to Yousef. "Look at the tape."

Yousef tries to grab the kid's elbow. "Sir—"

"No!" Denn, red-faced now, shrugs off Yousef's grasp. "Look at the goddamn tape! She"—jabbing his finger at Cattie—"and those two"—now pointing at Frisk and Morty—"set me up."

Morty, all indignation and injured pride, jumps up and starts shouting at Denn, and I think Denn is going to wade right through the table to go at Morty, but Yousef gets his skinny little body between them, and suddenly security is there, two hulking suits bookending the kid and lifting him off the carpet like he weighs nada. They haul him out of there, the kid shouting, "Look at the tape, Yousef!"

The funny thing is—maybe it's not so funny—is that the tape, assuming Yousef even looks at it, probably won't show a thing. Those security tapes don't pick up as much as you might think. However Cattie put that nine of clubs back into play, it was smooth. If neither Denn nor I saw her do it, odds are the tape won't show it either.

As soon as Denn is out of sight, this gray-faced dude in a matching thousand-dollar suit glides up out of nowhere. He comes up behind Cattie and puts his hands on her shoulders. She goes all stiff.

He looks at the cards on the table and smiles. "Bad beat?"

"I got lucky," says Frisk.

The gray guy nods, as if he's gotten what he came for, then lifts his hands from Cattie's shoulders and turns and fades back into the sea of slots.

Later on, back in my crib, I wonder why they went after the kid that way. There are bigger and easier fish in Vegas. Denn's lousy sixteen large is nothing to guys like that.

It had to be personal.

And I wonder about Cattie Hart. What would it

take to get her to drop a deck on a guy supposed to be her honey? All I can think is he must have done something really awful to piss her off that way.

And I was thinking I maybe might have said something about that nine of clubs I saw in Morty's hand, but in my world you don't play the other guy's game. You take care of numero uno, Bruno.

One player to a hand.

That's the way it is.

The way it's always been.

2

(Denn)

ONE HUNDRED DOLLARS AND EIGHTY-SEVEN cents. That was all of it. One fifty-dollar bill he had found in his wallet, tucked between his phony driver's license and his real one, the rest of it in small bills and coins gathered from pants pockets, the glove box of his Camaro, and under the sofa cushions.

Chump change.

Perched on a stool at the small counter in his kitchenette, Denn counted it three times. One hundred dollars and eighty-seven cents.

Denn stared down at the money, his features carefully blank. As long as he kept his face still, his eyes on the money, he would feel nothing. No despair, no joy, no fear, no heat. Just that cool, flat sense of the inevitable. Just another round of poker. He didn't have to think about where he had come from, where he was going, or who he was.

He did not have to think about Cattie.

All he had to think about was his next move: Fold, call, or raise?

Folding meant leaving Las Vegas. Denn closed his eyes and imagined himself back in Fairview, knocking on his mother's door. Going back to mowing lawns and trimming hedges for a living. He imagined his mother's face. It was a little fuzzy. He couldn't remember how she wore her hair. Would she recognize him? Would she want anything to do with him? Would she make him go back to finish high school?

He had left Fairview only a year ago, but it felt like a lifetime. Could he really go back?

Denn opened his eyes.

Fold, call, or raise?

He stacked the bills and coins. One fifty, four fives, twenty-seven ones, nine quarters, eight dimes, eleven nickels, and twenty-seven pennies. One hundred dollars and eighty-seven cents.

Again, he let his eyes fall shut. Faces swam into view, as crisp and clear as reality: Bill Frisk. Morty Deasel. Cattie.

His eyes snapped open.

One hundred dollars and eighty-seven cents. He rolled the ninety-seven dollars in paper money into a tight cylinder, wrapped it with a thick, blue rubber band, and stuffed the slim roll into his pocket. Then he scooped all the coins into his hand, walked around the counter, and dumped them into the trash.

Fold, call, or raise?

Sixty seconds later he was in his Camaro, heading southeast on the Boulder Highway.

Not thinking about Cattie.

3

(Denn)

THERE ARE STILL ROADS IN NEVADA WHERE A person can drive for an hour without seeing another human being.

But none of those roads are anywhere near Las Vegas.

Denn passed miles of apartment complexes, shopping centers, parking lots, and assorted fast-food restaurants. He drove past golf courses, gated housing developments, luxury resorts, and trailer parks. His body went on automatic, shifting gears and working the pedals without conscious thought.

There were exactly two places in the world where Denn felt like he belonged. One was at the poker table. The other was behind the wheel of his Camaro, driving fast, melting away the miles.

As he drove, his mind drifted back over the past

few months, gingerly probing his memories like a soldier sweeping a minefield.

Those first months in Vegas had been amazing. He had hit town with a hundred thousand in cash—the proceeds from selling Marcel's, the bar and restaurant he had won from Artie Kingston back in Fairview.

Denn sent his thoughts farther back into the past, to that night in the back room at Marcel's. His best night ever. The night he had watched "the King" slowly unravel during a marathon game of holdem. Denn had gone into that game with a few thousand dollars, and had come out of it owning the joint. Sixteen years old. Not even old enough to sell himself a drink, and he had won himself a nightclub.

Denn would always remember the last thing Artie Kingston had said to him.

They had been in Artie's lawyer's office. Artie had just signed over the title of his restaurant. Denn, feeling awkward, had said, "That was some game."

Artie gave him a flat, humorless smile.

"It's not over till you're dead, kid. It's all one big game."

Denn smiled, shaking his head. He had never wanted to own a bar and restaurant. All he'd ever wanted to do was play cards.

Within a few months Marcel's had lost half its business due to neglectful management, and then the state yanked the liquor license because he was underage. He sold the place for cheap, a hundred grand, to his restaurant manager, a guy named Sicard, and headed for Vegas, the poker capital of the known universe.

He wondered now whether Sicard had purposely let the restaurant fail so that he could buy it cheap.

And he wondered where Sicard had gotten the money to buy it.

The first thing Denn had done in Vegas was head down to the poker room at the Bellagio and take a seat in the biggest game going that night: a $400-$800 mixed game—a round of holdem, a round of Omaha high-low, and a round of deuce-to-seven triple draw. He recognized a couple of the other players from poker magazines: Jen Harman and Daniel Negreanu. The other four at the table he didn't know, but they all played like they knew what they were doing. One of them, Sammy Gold, had the longest canine teeth Denn had ever seen on a human being. The way Sammy looked at him made Denn feel like a lamb staring down the throat of a timber wolf.

He had never before faced competition like this.

Artie Kingston had been good, but that bunch made the King look like a small-town amateur.

Denn's first night at the Bellagio had been educational. He started out playing his usual game—tight before the flop, then balls-out aggressive on the later streets—and dropped $13,000 in the first hour.

Those guys were good.

Denn figured he could be better.

He learned quickly. Slumped in his seat, cap pulled low over his eyes, sunglasses dark as obsidian, fingers nimbly fingering his chips, he watched. He learned how they held their hands. How they bet. Who was weak. Who was strong. Watching for tells, seeing how the money flowed, blocking out the deceptive banter with his iPod, sinking into the matrix of odds and personalities and opportunities.

Players and cards and chips came and went, and by the third night he began to win.

One night, Denn caught a trey on the river to scoop a $7500 Omaha pot. The new player to his left, a young, long-haired guy wearing a bowler hat, turned to him and said, "Dude, you're killing me."

"Sorry," Denn said.

"No, you're not."

Denn laughed. "Where'd you get the hat?"

"EBay." He held out a hand. "Jimbo Cowles."

"Denn Doyle." They shook hands.

"Look out, Jimbo," said Sammy Gold. "Kid's luckier'n a double-dicked rooster in a henhouse.

Denn smiled. Unlike Sammy, he didn't believe in luck. What he believed was that every time Sammy had a big hand, his nostrils flared slightly. And when Sammy was bluffing, he always hesitated slightly before betting, just the tiniest fraction of a second, as if to keep himself from betting too fast.

The other players had their tells too. In time Denn learned them all. The other regulars began, grudgingly, to respect him as their equal.

He settled into a routine. During the day he slept. It was a good life. He never thought about the future. Everything was about the cards.

Until he met Cattie Hart.

4

(Cattie)

FOR AS LONG AS SHE COULD REMEMBER, Cattie Hart had been angry.

Even before she could remember: According to her mother she had emerged from the womb screaming like a horror-movie starlet, had howled and spat through her first four years, and had been kicked out of kindergarten the first day for stabbing a classmate with a pair of safety scissors.

Cattie didn't remember that, but she believed it.

Reaching into her purse, she touched the gold-bead necklace that had once belonged to Denn Doyle. She would keep it to remind herself of how much it could hurt to trust someone—especially her—and how dangerous it was to love.

"Little warm-up, honey?" asked the waitress, her voice pitched high to cut through the background jangle of the slot machines. The café was tucked in the back corner of the Slot Paradise, one of the seedier casinos on the Strip. Cattie, still wearing her dealer outfit from the Sand Dunes, was the only customer.

She nodded without looking up, then watched fresh coffee stream from the pot into her cup. She always drank it black. The bitter, sour heat of it made her feel righteous. And black was her color.

As a teenager, Cattie had withdrawn into a scowling black funk. Literally black. She had dyed her red hair black. Black clothes, black eye shadow, black lipstick, black nails. The kids at school called her a goth, but she wasn't goth, and she didn't care what they thought. She had no friends and no dreams. Life was just a contemptible train of stupid, selfish people hell-bent on destroying themselves and every other living thing on the planet. The closest Cattie came to having a goal in life was the desire to let everyone she came into contact with know they were doomed, worthless losers.

Everyone, even her mother—*especially* her mother—had been relieved when she'd left Aitken, Minnesota.

After that, six months in L.A., eight weeks at a Las Vegas dealer school, six months dealing poker at Casino Arizona in Phoenix, and another six months dealing blackjack at a succession of gambling halls all over Nevada. It was during that time that she'd learned how to work a deck of cards from Ginny Geertz, a dealer she'd shared an apartment with in Reno. Ginny had taught Cattie false cuts, dealing seconds and bottoms, peeks, crimps, holdouts, and several other techniques. Cattie had been an eager student—not so much because she wanted to cheat, but because she wanted to be in control. She wanted the cards to do what she wanted. And they did.

A few months later, bored with dealing, she found herself working the other side of the black-jack tables in Lake Tahoe with Jerry Burkhardt, a small-time card counter. Jerry was a moron, but he taught her a few things.

Around that time she abandoned her goth look and went back to her natural hair color, a solid Irish red. The fresh, natural look appealed to men. They thought it made her look trustworthy and innocent.

Men were idiots. All of them.

"What's the matter, doll?"

Cattie looked up. "Hey, Morty, I was just think-ing about you."

Morty Deasel fitted his bulky body into the other side of the vinyl booth. Cattie sipped her coffee and waited.

"Heard Yousef let you go," Morty said.

"What did you expect? You think Jimbo Cowles

or Del the Cabby would ever sit down at another game with me dealing?"

Morty shrugged and pulled a pack of Camels from the breast pocket of his shirt, black with orange polka dots. "They couldn't prove nothing. I figured they'd give you the benefit of the doubt."

"This is Vegas, Morty. There is no benefit of the doubt."

Morty shrugged and lit his cigarette. "What the hell, kid. Moves like you got, you can get another job in a Las Vegas minute. Fact is, the man might just have something for you over at the Crossing."

"Would I have to work with you?"

"You know you love the action, kiddo."

Cattie gave him her best blank stare—the look that made most people squirm. But Morty just looked straight back at her and laughed smoke.

"You are one hard-ass little bitch, ain'tcha."

"You going to give me my money, Morty?"

Morty smiled and stared at her with his piggy little eyes. Cattie let him look, giving him nothing, letting him know she didn't give a crap what he did.

And the truth was, she really didn't. If he gave her the money, she'd find something to do with it. If he didn't give it to her, then that was no more than she deserved. It would serve her right. Because as much as Cattie Hart wanted to punish all of humanity, she wanted to punish herself more.

Morty finally shrugged and reached into his back pocket. He came out with a thick roll of bills and thumped it onto the table.

"There ya go, little Judas. Ten K. You want to count it?" He drew on his cigarette.

Cattie picked up the roll of hundreds and dropped it into her purse.

"I trust you, Morty."

He squinted at her through the cloud of blue smoke. "You do?"

"As much as I trust anyone," she said as she slid out of the booth and walked out of the café without looking back.

5

(Jimbo)

IT CAN BE A THING OF BEAUTY, OR IT CAN BE
ugly as roadkill, depending which side of the bet
you got. I'm talking about luck, Chuck.

I've seen a guy lose for years and then all of a
sudden one day the gods bless the shit out of him
and he can't lose for trying.

Of course, mostly it goes the other way. A guy is
doing okay, playing pretty good, making a few
bucks—and then he has a bad run. It happens to all
of us. So the guy hunkers down, playing his game
the best he can, waiting patiently for his luck to
change . . . and then it don't. And the guy thinks,
how many times can my pocket aces get cracked?
How many times can my nut flush lose to a full
house? How many times can I lose to a two-outer on
the river?

And then something pops, and you can smell it

all up and down the Strip. The guy starts chasing his luck; he goes full tilt boogie and it's all over, Rover.

But I didn't think it would happen that way to Denn Doyle.

Denn was a prodigy, one of those guys you swear has got X-ray vision and a supercomputer for a brain. The kid was stone cold focused, imaginative, and fearless. He was the Cincinnati Kid, only for real. Stu Ungar, but without the cocaine and the attitude. Johnny Moss with shades and an iPod.

But you know how it is. In the poker world, when you think something could never possibly happen, it does. I was there the day the kid's luck changed—and it wasn't that game where he got cheated by Morty and Frisk and Cattie. That was just the coo-de-grass, as they say.

The night the kid's luck turned happened two weeks before that, also at the Sand Dunes. Cattie was dealing. Of course, I didn't know her at the time, and neither did Denn. And I didn't think nothing of it, either. The kid lost one hand. No biggie. But now, looking back, I think it was a sign as big as the Hoover Dam. Sam.

6

(Denn)

THE TRAFFIC THINNED; SUBURBAN SPRAWL gave way to desert bleak. Denn shut off the air-conditioning, lowered all the windows, and let the hot, dry air roar through the car, willing it to rip away his thoughts.

It didn't work.

Cattie Hart.

Cattie Hart.

Cattie Hart.

He kept seeing her face, the look she had given him over that nine of clubs. What had it been? Triumph? Regret? Delight? Embarrassment?

He didn't know.

Denn could sit down at a poker table with a complete stranger, and twenty minutes later he could read him like a neon sign. He'd known Cattie for two weeks, and it was like trying to read a bare concrete wall.

Two weeks?

It felt like a lifetime.

Two weeks ago he'd built his bankroll up to $268,000. He was playing in a little $100 entry, no-limit holdem tournament at the Dunes, just for fun. First place was worth $7000.

Denn had caught a few good hands early, then tightened up his game and watched the other players knock each other off. Four hours into the tournament most of the players had been eliminated, and they were down to two tables. Denn had $20,000 in tournament chips, slightly more than average.

The tournament was strictly small-time. It was a weak field—mostly tourists. Other than Denn, there were no top pros. A $100 buy-in tournament simply isn't rich enough to interest serious players.

"Dude, you slummin?"

Denn turned and looked up at the long-haired, bowler-hatted guy standing behind him. Jimbo Cowles, the closest thing he had to a friend in Vegas.

"Hey, Jimbo," Denn said. "You in this thing?"

"You know I don't play the babies," Jimbo said. "What are you doing here?"

Denn shrugged. "Got a free entry."

"Free?" Jimbo laughed. "Nothin' free in this town."

"Seriously. I was in the rest room at the Bellagio, and the guy at the urinal next to me says he bought a ticket into this tournament, only he has to catch a flight back to Boise, so he asks me if I want it. For free. What the hell. A hundred bucks is a hundred bucks, right?"

Jimbo shook his head doubtfully. "Maybe," he said as Denn looked at his next hand and mucked it. "But I wouldn't bet on it."

Right about then Denn caught his first look at Cattie Hart.

She had just sat down to deal at the next table over. The first thing he saw was her long red hair.

For a few seconds he forgot about Jimbo, forgot about the game, forgot about everything but that red hair. And those burnt-caramel eyes that sat a little tilted on her face, like maybe she had one Asian grandmother and one Irish. She looked too young to be dealing.

"Dude!"

Denn snapped out of it. "What?"

"You having an episode?"

Denn pointed his chin at the redhead. "You know her?"

Jimbo shook his hair off his face and squinted. "Her? I seen her around. Her name's Cattie something. Don't really know her, though."

"She looks like somebody I used to know." *In another life,* he thought, reaching up to touch his gold necklace. He tried to remember exactly what Kelly Rollingate had looked like, but all he could remember was the red hair and caramel eyes.

Jimbo snorted. "Yeah, she looks like somebody you'd *like* to know. Better play your hand, dude."

Denn looked at his cards. Pocket nines. "That's not what I meant," he said, raising $3000.

The player to his left, a tourist wearing a Jack Daniel's T-shirt, frowned at his cards, shook his head sadly, sighed, shrugged, then raised all-in.

Denn smiled at the tourist's transparent act. The guy obviously had a monster hand—aces or kings. Denn threw his nines into the muck. The tourist smiled sheepishly, and turned up a pair of aces.

"Good fold," he said.

Half an hour later they were down to the final table. Denn had $91,000 in tournament chips, giving him a comfortable lead over most of the other players. Only the tourist in the Jack Daniel's T-shirt had him out-chipped.

Denn knew how to play it—tight as a fist until three or four players have been eliminated, then loosen up and start buying a few pots. Hit the small stacks hard, and avoid heads-up confrontations with the big ones. Don't do anything stupid. Don't risk it all on a hand that is only a five to four favorite. Wait for the best price.

He figured he was a big favorite to win first place.

The redhead—Cattie—was dealing. Denn, hidden behind his shades, watched her hands on the cards. She was good, as smooth and fast as any dealer he'd seen. The cards sailed low across the table with machine-gun rapidity. Denn appreciated talent. He admired people who were the best at whatever they chose to be. He imagined her hands touching him.

She dealt him a pair of queens, two black ladies. Denn raised. The next three players folded; then the tourist in the Jack Daniel's T-shirt shook his head, sighed, shrugged, and shoved all his chips into the middle of the table.

Denn stared at the pile of chips, then took a good look at the bettor. The last time that guy had shaken his head like that, sighed, then gone all-in, he'd had pocket aces. But did it follow that he'd do exactly the same thing twice? Maybe this time it was a bluff. Maybe the guy had something like a pair of tens and he was just trying to shut Denn out of the pot to pro-tect his hand. Maybe he was thinking that Denn would remember how he'd bet his aces before, and would assume that he had another monster. Was he that sophisticated?

If the guy had pocket aces or pocket kings, Denn would be almost dead: With only two queens left in the deck, his chance of beating a bigger pocket pair was only about one in five.

But if the guy had anything less—a semi-bluff with ace, king . . . ace, queen suited . . . pocket babies . . . something like that—or if he was making some sort of insane bluff with a deuce, seven—then Denn would be a huge favorite.

"It's on you," Cattie said to Denn, caramel eyes piercing his sunglasses.

Denn stared at the tourist. If he called and won, it would give him the biggest stack at the table—a huge advantage. If he lost, he'd be busted out of the tournament.

Denn's eyes flicked to Cattie, who was watching him with a faint smile.

Denn knew he should fold. The guy could have aces. He should wait for a better chance, and that chance would come if he let it. But something in Cattie's smile made him think that she wanted him to call. And if he called, and the guy had crap, think how good he'd look. How smart.

What the hell, he thought.

"I call." He showed his pocket queens. The guy in the Tigers cap smiled and turned up his hand. Pocket aces. Again. Denn felt his stomach drop right through his chair. *Stupid, stupid, stupid.*

"Nice hand," he said, his voice a croak. He stood up, getting ready to leave.

Cattie flopped three cards—deuce, nine, nine—followed by a jack and then, just to rub salt in it, an ace. Denn, trying to control his shaking hands, walked over to the tournament director to claim his tenth-place winnings, a lousy three hundred bucks.

An hour later, sitting in the café nursing a Coke, he looked up to see Cattie standing beside his table.

"Sorry about those aces," she said.

"Not your fault," he said.

"Always blame it on the dealer. Didn't they teach you that at poker camp?"

Denn laughed. "My name's Denn," he said.

"I know who you are. You've been tearing up the tables in this town. You've got the old pros all shaking their heads."

"I guess I've been lucky."

"You believe in luck?"

"Sure I do," Denn said. "You're standing here talking to me. I feel lucky."

Cattie gave him a hard smile and looked away. "Luck comes in two flavors. Maybe I'm the kind you don't want."

"Maybe," said Denn.

"My name's Cattie."

"I know," he said, pointing at her badge.

"No you don't," she said, unclipping the badge from her blouse. "You don't know anything about me."

Denn lifted his foot from the accelerator. The Camaro slowed to ninety, eighty-five, eighty. He set the cruise control at a sedate seventy-five miles per hour and rolled up the windows.

Cattie had been right. He hadn't known anything about her then, and he knew nothing about her now. Other than the fact that for some reason she had set out to destroy him.

He did know one thing, though.

He needed to know *why.*

7

(Cattie)

CATTIE HART TOOK THE $10,000 MORTY PAID her and used it to prop up the short leg of the crappy little table in her crappy little kitchenette in her crappy little furnished apartment off Duval Street.

Vegas was full of streets like Duval. Cheap apartment complexes built in the eighties and nineties, a few hundred bucks a month, apartments full of single people from Cincinnati and Minneapolis and Buffalo and Albuquerque come to Vegas to make their fortune gambling, dealing, pouring drinks, waiting tables, picking pockets—it was all the same action as far as Cattie was concerned. Crappy little people making a crappy little living off the tourist trade, like fleas on a big shaggy dog.

The table felt nice and solid with the half inch-thick wad of hundreds under the far left leg. Cattie poured a ginger ale into her wineglass, the only glass she owned. She had grabbed it from Patsy's of Naples the night of her first date with Denn. A souvenir. Cattie was big on souvenirs. Her apartment was full of ashtrays and saltshakers and anything else she could slip into her purse. But she only had that one wineglass.

Cattie thought back to that first date.

Denn had seemed so young. When he was playing poker, all frozen-faced and mysterious behind his ultradark shades, Denn looked to be in his midtwenties or even older. But sitting in the red leatherette booth at the back of Patsy's, drinking Coca-Cola instead of wine, fumbling with his utensils, and struggling to make conversation, he had seemed like a kid.

At first he had just wanted to talk poker, as if he didn't know anything else to talk about. Denn Doyle had a remarkable memory for poker hands. He remembered not only the cards, but the betting sequences of every hand and the mannerisms of the other players.

"There isn't a high-stakes player in Vegas I don't have a tell on," he had boasted.

"Like what?" she'd asked.

"Well, Sammy Gold—he plays in the big game at the Bellagio—he always hesitates a beat before he tries a bluff. And when he's got a big hand, he flares his nostrils. Just a little." Denn demonstrated. "And Jimmy the Swede has these false teeth he's always clacking—except when he really likes his hand, then the clacking stops. Pretty much all of them have some little thing they do, or don't do, that tells me something about what they got."

"Do they have tells on you?" Cattie asked.

"They just see me as a kid wearing shades and an iPod."

"So how old are you?" Cattie watched him wrap his fork in linguini.

Denn looked at her and grinned.

Cattie sat back, genuinely surprised. "Oh my God, you're not even legal, are you?" In Las Vegas, legal age for gambling is twenty-one.

Denn put his forefinger to his lips.

Cattie laughed. "So what are you? Nineteen?"

Denn fitted an enormous forkful of linguini into his mouth and stared back at her, chewing.

"Eighteen?" Cattie said.

Denn swallowed his linguini.

"Not quite," he said.

Cattie wasn't sure which surprised her more— that Denn was only seventeen years old, or that he had admitted it. Her own policy was to never tell anybody anything she didn't need them to know. For example, her fake California driver's license stated her age as twenty-two. Which was three years older than her true age of nineteen. She was still a teenager, but not one other person in the entire state of Nevada knew it.

Information was power, and Cattie did not give away power easily.

Denn, for all his brilliant play at the poker table, was puppy dog naive. She could hardly believe he had told her about the tells he had gathered on the other high-stakes players.

She had given him a chance. That first date, she told him some things about herself. Things that would have scared any normal guy away. She told him that she was dangerous, that she couldn't be trusted, that all she wanted to do in her life was play the angles and stick it to anybody who gave her the opportunity.

"I don't care what you've done," he said.

"I'm a stone cold bee-yatch," she said.

Denn had laughed. Like she couldn't hurt him. Or wouldn't.

Cattie sipped her wineglass of ginger ale, wishing it were vodka. Liquor made some people feel better—for a while. She saw it all the time in the casinos: Miserable, unhappy people would start throwing down drinks, and suddenly they seemed happy.

Happy to lose their money. But when Cattie drank alcohol, all that happened was that she got dizzy and sad. Dizzy and sad was no fun, so she didn't drink. But sometimes she wished she could, just to make it all go away for a time.

Her purse began to shiver and buzz. Cattie opened it and took out her cell phone.

"Hello?"

"Catherine." A voice as flat and lifeless as a machine's.

"Oh. Hi."

"You did good, kid."

"Don't sound so surprised."

"Do I sound surprised?"

"Actually, you don't even sound like you're alive."

"Ha. Ha. Ha." That was how he laughed. "Morty told me you were in a pissy mood."

"It's more like a permanent condition."

"Sorry to hear that. Catherine, how would you feel about another job?"

"No, thanks."

He didn't say anything.

After several seconds passed, Cattie said, "What is it?"

He laughed. "Ha. Ha. Ha."

8

(Denn)

WHILE LAS VEGAS IS A SHRINE TO FRIVOLITY and disposability, Hoover Dam is a monument to solidity and permanence. Denn parked his car and walked out onto the enormous concrete structure. Tall as a seventy-story building and weighing in at nearly seven million tons, the dam seemed to have a gravity of its own, sucking at the soles of Denn's black K-Swiss sneakers.

He had been there before. Several times. Hoover Dam, one of the seven wonders of the modern world, was less than an hour from Vegas.

Standing against the rail on the downstream side, Denn stared down the sloping concrete face of the dam to the brown, roiling waters seven hundred feet below. He could sense the millions of kilowatt-hours of electricity being produced daily within the dam's power plants—enough to light up the city of

Las Vegas, the most lightbulb-infested city on earth, with enough juice left over to light up most of Arizona.

Sometimes at the poker table Denn imagined himself as the dam, rock solid and humming with repressed energy. Standing atop the dam had once made him feel both tiny and powerful. Tiny because the dam was so huge. Powerful because Denn knew that men—human beings—had conceived, planned, and built the thing. But now, staring down at the turgid, foamy waters, he felt as vulnerable as a pair of deuces.

Thirty-eight men had died building the dam. They were more than seventy years gone now, but they had left something behind. They were remembered. Every time a tourist visited the great concrete structure and read the bronze plaques and marveled at the sheer size and ambition of the project, those thirty-eight men were remembered.

What was *he* building? A reputation? A rep as a kid who had ruled the poker tables for a few short months, then flamed out over a girl?

Again, he found himself thinking about Cattie. Was it something he had done? Or had she been out to get him from the beginning?

He thought back over the past two weeks, beginning with the little tournament where he'd first met

Cattie. Two straight weeks of losses. He'd lost one heart and a quarter of a million dollars.

Had Cattie engineered the whole thing?

Denn couldn't see how.

It was his own damned fault. He'd let her in.

He'd let himself fall in love.

9

(Jimbo)

LET ME TELL YOU ABOUT LOVE. I'VE SEEN A few guys could handle it, but I've seen more guys, they fall for some piece of ass, and next thing you know they crumble like a stale Oreo. Love and poker don't mix. It's like trying to eat a pizza and do jumping jacks at the same time. A guy that brings his relationship to the table is burnt toast. And vice versa, I suppose—you start bending some chick's ear with your pathetic bad-beat stories, you might as well be picking your nose at the dinner table.

Now I'm no rocket surgeon, but I could see that happening to Denn as soon as he and Cattie got to be an item. He slid into that big game over at the Bellagio with his head full of Cattie, and those guys saw it right away. He was meat on a platter. He was cooked. He was roadkill, Bill.

10

(Cattie)

"CAN I SEE THAT ONE?" CATTIE POINTED AT A diamond and ruby pendant.

"Certainly," said the salesclerk. She spread a square of velvet fabric over the glass countertop, lifted the pendant from the case, and laid it on the black velvet. Cattie held it up to her neck, noting the tiny price tag as she did so: $9,700.

"What do you think?" she asked the clerk.

"It looks lovely on you."

Cattie smiled and asked to see another item, a small emerald brooch.

"Certainly, miss."

Cattie loved shopping for jewelry in Las Vegas. Anywhere else she would have been treated with suspicion or, at best, condescension. But in Vegas the store clerks were well aware that anybody, no matter their age, dress, or grammar, might have just hit a million-dollar jackpot.

Cattie looked at a pair of $8,000 diamond earrings, tried on a white gold and sapphire bracelet, and compared several pearl necklaces at prices ranging from $400 to $5,000. She had ten thousand dollars cash in her purse. She could buy almost any item in the Bloomingdale's jewelry department.

After twenty minutes of keeping the clerk scurrying about, Cattie announced that she just couldn't make up her mind.

"I'll have to come back later," she said. "With my husband."

The clerk smiled her most patient and professional smile. "We're open until eleven tonight," she said.

"I'll be back." Cattie made her way quickly through the store and out the entrance. She waited until she reached her car to look at the ruby earrings she had stolen. She adjusted the rearview mirror and put them on. The earrings were beautiful, but they didn't work with her red hair. Oh, well.

She noticed a young man walking to his car carrying a Macy's bag. Cattie rolled down her window.

"Hey!"

The young man looked at her.

"You have a girlfriend?" Cattie asked.

"Uh . . . yeah?"

"Come here." She held out her hand, showing him the earrings. "Give her these. She'll be thrilled."

The young man looked at the earrings. "Are they real?"

"Of course they are."

"What do you want for them?"

"Nothing. It's free earring day at the mall. Take them. Merry Christmas. Happy birthday. Whatever."

The young man, looking very confused, took the earrings. Cattie started her car and drove off. When she got home, she put the sheaf of hundred dollar bills, still $10,000, back under the table leg.

Her cell phone buzzed.

Cattie checked the caller ID. She frowned. Denn. Again. Why didn't he just give up and go back to Fairview? She held the phone in her hand, feeling the vibrations, waiting for the buzzing and shivering to stop.

The afternoon of the day after their first date, Cattie had taken Denn to one of her favorite places in all of Las Vegas: the top of the Stratosphere Tower, the tallest building west of the Mississippi.

"I can't believe you've never been up here," she said as they rode up the double-decker elevator to the top of the tower.

"I've been kind of busy," Denn said.

"What have you done besides play poker?"

Denn shrugged. "Not much."

The night before, Denn had told Cattie the story of his life. How he had been a kid in Fairview, living with his screwed-up mom, mowing lawns for pocket money.

"Poker was the best thing that ever happened to me," he told her. "Except that I lost all my friends and my mom kicked me out, but that was okay. Not much action in Fairview anyways."

"Not like here," Cattie said as the elevator sighed to a stop.

"Not like here," Denn agreed. He followed Cattie out of the elevator.

They stepped out onto a wide deck encircling the outside edge of the flying saucer-shaped top of the tower. Denn walked straight to the railing and looked out over the city.

"How high are we?" he asked.

"I think it's about a thousand feet."

"I wonder if anybody's ever BASE-jumped from here."

"This is Las Vegas. Somebody's done everything from everywhere."

Denn looked around. "I thought there was a roller coaster up here."

"They took it down," Cattie said. "But they have something better now."

There were three thrill rides atop the tower, and Cattie had ridden all of them. The Big Shot was a vertical ride that climbed more than one hundred feet up the mast, then dropped back to observation-deck level. The newest ride, Insanity, dangled riders out over the edge of the tower at the end of five long arms. The arms would rotate faster and faster, splaying outward as they picked up speed. The peak of the ride came when you were pressed into your seat at three g's looking straight down at the Strip.

That was a pretty good ride. But Cattie's favorite ride was the X Scream.

"Close your eyes," she said.

Denn closed his eyes. Cattie led him by the hand around the observation deck to the X Scream.

The X Scream was a ramp sticking up at an angle over the edge of the deck. Cattie handed the ride boy their tickets, helped Denn climb into one of the eight orange plastic chairs at the lower end of the ramp, and locked him in. She got into the seat next to him.

"Okay, you can look now."

Denn opened his eyes and looked around. Sixty feet of ramp stretched out before them, angled up into the pale blue sky.

"What does it do?"

She reached over and took his hand. "Wait for it."

They began to rise, the ramp tipping like a giant teeter-totter.

Denn said, "Does it spin around or something?"

"Not exactly."

When the teeter-totter reached its maximum height, they were looking down a steeply sloped ramp.

"What does—"

Cattie smiled as the car suddenly broke free. They were sliding down the ramp at tremendous speed. She heard Denn gasp. The car hit the end of the ramp, and the padded steel restraining bar bit into her belly as they came to an abrupt halt, dangling over the edge of the tower, nothing but a thousand feet of air between them and the hard asphalt streets of Vegas.

She looked at Denn. His eyes were huge, his mouth gaping in a silent scream.

They began to rise, the teeter-totter returning to its original position.

Denn looked at her, his mouth opening and closing like a fish gasping for water.

"Want to go again?" she asked.

Denn nodded and found his voice.

"As many times as you want."

11

(Denn)

DENN LEANED OVER THE RAILING STARING down at the muddy, roiling waters at the base of the dam, remembering.

The night after his ride with Cattie on the X Scream, he had sat down at the Bellagio with the usual crew. They were playing deuce-to-seven triple draw, $1000-$2000 limit. Triple draw wasn't Denn's best game, but he could hold his own. He would play tight, protecting his stack, until the other players got bored and decided to go back to playing holdem, his best game.

He plugged in his iPod, lowered the visor of his cap, and settled in.

In deuce-to-seven triple draw, hands are ranked the opposite of regular poker. The best possible hand was two, three, four, five, seven, not all of the same suit. A royal flush was utterly worthless. Four aces were just as bad.

So, as sometimes happened, Denn started getting dealt a series of incredible but worthless hands: trip aces, king-high flush, a straight to the ace, and so forth. All he could do was fold, fold, fold, and fold.

Passing up hand after hand, he kept thinking about his date with Cattie. The way her eyes looked in candlelight. Her hands. The spray of freckles across the tops of her breasts. The feeling of having her next to him; her smell. They had gone for a ride in the desert. *Go faster,* she had said. *Faster.* He had brought the Camaro up over a hundred miles per hour and held it there, wondering what a jackrabbit or coyote could do to his car at that speed.

And then the ride that afternoon on the X Scream, dangling a thousand feet above the Strip, holding her hand.

Another hand appeared before him: two, three, four, jack, king. He shook off the memories. He had three draws to turn that king-jack into something better. Sammy Gold bet $1000. Denn raised. Everybody else folded.

Sammy shook his head and called Denn's raise. "I don't know why I bother with you, kid. You always win."

Denn discarded his king, jack and drew a seven, nine, giving him a nine high. Not bad, but not great.

He imagined Cattie standing behind him with her hand on his shoulder, watching him.

Sammy stood pat, choosing not to draw; then he checked.

Denn bet. He imagined the corners of Cattie's wide mouth turning up, admiring his reckless courage.

Sammy raised.

Denn reraised.

Sammy kicked him back again.

Denn sat back in his chair and considered his situation. Clearly, Sammy thought he had a pretty good hand—probably an eight-high, maybe something like an eight, seven, or an eight, six. To beat him, Denn would have to discard his nine and draw a five, a six, or an eight. Twelve cards that could help him out of forty-five. About one in four. With more than $10,000 in the pot, it was worth calling the $2000 raise, so he did.

Again, Sammy chose not to draw. Denn discarded his nine and drew an eight, giving him an 8, 7, 4, 3, 2. Not bad.

Sammy bet $2000.

Denn raised.

Sammy reraised.

Denn hesitated. Could Sammy have a monster? He was sure betting like he did.

Again Denn felt Cattie's presence. He raised.

Sammy raised him back.

Denn sat back in his chair and considered his situation. He couldn't see a guy like Sammy Gold shoving all those bets into the pot without at least an eight, six. Or maybe even an eight, five. Either of which would beat Denn's eight, seven.

But he had one more draw. He called.

Sammy stood pat, passing up his last chance to draw a card.

Denn stared at his hand. If he discarded the eight and drew a five, he would have seven, five, four, three, two. The absolute nuts. If he drew a six, that would be almost as good. Anything else, he was toast. The question was, did Sammy have his eight, seven beat?

Denn closed his eyes. When faced with a tough decision, he sometimes imagined that he was watching himself. If he made the wrong choice, then so be it. It would only matter to him. But now all he could think about was how Cattie would see him. She wasn't really there, but he could almost feel her brown nails digging into his shoulder.

Sammy had to have his eight, seven beat.

With eight cards that could help him in the deck, Denn decided to go for it. He discarded the eight.

The dealer tossed Denn a card.

Denn lifted the corner of the fresh card and looked at it. The king of clubs. His hand was all but worthless.

Sammy bet $2000.

Denn sat as if paralyzed and stared at the king in his hand.

He looked up.

Sammy smiled, showing Denn those ridiculously long canine teeth. Were his nostrils flared?

Yes, they were.

And Sammy only flared his nostrils when he was sitting on the nuts.

How had he not seen that before?

No point in throwing good money after bad. Even with close to $20,000 in the pot, he couldn't call Sammy's $2000 bet. He tossed his cards into the muck.

Sammy's smile widened.

"Good one, kid." He turned up his cards: ace, ace, ace, jack, jack.

Everyone at the table—except Denn—burst into laughter. Sammy had stood pat for all three draws with one of the worst starting hands possible, and he had gotten Denn to throw away the winner.

"What did you throw away there, kid?"

Denn shook his head, refusing to answer, going

back over the hand in his mind. How had he misread Sammy? Had Sammy figured out that Denn had figured out his tells? Or had Denn been so busy thinking about Cattie that he'd gotten them mixed up?

He couldn't remember.

Things did not improve for him that night. The loss to Sammy threw Denn off his game. The other players smelled it on him like sharks smell blood, and for the rest of the night it was open season on Denn, who couldn't win a hand to save his life.

He lost nearly $80,000 in that one session.

He couldn't really blame that one on Cattie, Denn thought as he stared down the sloping face of the Hoover Dam. She hadn't even been there. It had been his own stupidity that had cost him that night.

And the next night.

And the night after that.

Even then Denn hadn't quite understood that he was at the front end of the worst losing streak of his life. He thought it was just a couple of unlucky breaks. In poker that happens. He always knew that he would hit a losing streak sooner or later. That didn't make it any easier. But he never thought he would keep on losing.

So he spent his days with Cattie, taking in the tourist sights in Vegas. She took him to the Liberace

Museum to see the late entertainer's collection of bejeweled and bedecked grand pianos, cars, and costumes. "This is the real Las Vegas," she said. "Jewel-encrusted dead things."

They visited the Madame Tussaud's wax museum, where Cattie told him that she envied the wax figures. "They look so peaceful," she said.

They spent an afternoon at Mandalay Bay's Shark Reef, watching the sharks swimming in the glass-sided 1.6 million-gallon tank. "I think I played holdem with that one," said Denn, pointing at a particularly large hammerhead.

Nights, Cattie worked as a dealer at the Sand Dunes. Denn played poker. He lost. In that one week he lost more than $230,000 dollars to the boys at the Bellagio. Somehow he had gone from being a member of the wolf pack to being the lamb. He was down to his last $16,000.

"It comes and goes," Cattie had said, snuggled up against him on his rented leather sofa, comforting him after his fifth night of losses.

"Yeah, well, lately it's mostly been going. Like all of a sudden the rules changed."

"Maybe they've got a tell on you."

"Maybe."

"Sometimes when you touch that necklace of yours, I think it means you're worried."

"I don't do that at the card table." His hand drifted up to touch the chain of gold beads, the necklace he had bought for Kelly, his girlfriend back in Fairview. The gift she had rejected just before dumping him. He ran his thumb over the beads of gold.

"Why do you wear it? You don't seem like a jewelry guy."

"I'm not." Why *did* he wear it? It only reminded him of one of the worst days of his life. He pulled the necklace up over his head. "Do you like it?"

"Is it real gold?"

Denn nodded.

"I like it," Cattie said.

"It's yours."

Cattie held the necklace in her hand and looked at it for a long time. "Are you sure?"

"It hasn't brought me any luck lately."

Instead of putting it around her neck, Cattie dribbled the necklace into her purse.

"Maybe you should try a different game," she said.

"Like what? Golf?"

"I mean a different casino."

"I suppose," said Denn glumly.

"We're spreading no-limit now down at the Sand Dunes."

Denn snorted. "Yeah, right. A little hundred-dollar buy-in game isn't going to do me any good."

"We get some bigger games sometimes. You want me to call you if we get something going?"

Denn shrugged.

The next day she called him on his cell, and Denn took his last $16,000 to the Sand Dunes, where he met Bill Frisk and Morty Deasel.

12

(Jimbo)

I GOT A RULE. ANYBODY RINGS MY CELL before noon, I probably don't want to talk to them, so I answer in Mexican. Usually they hang up. Unless they're Mexican, and then *I* hang up on *them*, on account of I don't know any Mexicans except for a few poker players, and they know better than to call before noon. Also, I don't really know how to talk Mexican.

So when my cell rings and it's like ten to twelve, even though I'm awake I say, *"Hola, Margarita."*

"Jimbo, it's me."

"Buenos freaking *días. Dónde está la* freaking *baño. Hasta la* freaking *vista, enchilada con queso. Por qué vamanos, muy—"*

"Cut it out, Jimbo. It's me, Denn."

"Denn, dude! *¿Cómo está?"*

"Do you even know what you're saying?"

"No way, José. How you doing?"

"How do you think?"

"That was raw sewage, man."

"You saw it, right?"

"The nine of clubs?" I saw it all right. "Yeah, I saw it."

"Thanks for speaking up."

"Dude!"

"I know, I know—you weren't in the hand."

That's a thing you might not understand if you aren't a poker player. At the poker table I would check-raise Denn for his last ten bucks. But away from the table we're tight.

I can hear him breathing, and what sounds like wind in the background.

"Where you calling from?" I ask.

"Hoover Dam."

"Dude! Not gonna jump, are you?"

"Nah. I'm a lousy swimmer."

"Very funny. So what did you do to her?"

Denn doesn't say anything for a few seconds, then he says, "You mean Cattie."

"Yeah, I mean Cattie. What did you do to piss her off?"

"I don't know. I thought we were good."

"Dude. You got to talk to her."

"I tried to call her. She won't answer her phone."

"Go see her," I say.

"Is she still working at the Dunes?"

"Yousef fired her after . . . well, you know."

Again, I hear nada but wind. I change the subject.

"Hey, you hear about the Big Deal?" I ask.

"What's that?"

"You know King's Crossing, that new joint off Sahara?"

"Place looks like a Kmart?"

"Yeah, that's it. They opened a new poker room, and they're having this grand-opening tournament next week. Calling it 'the Big Deal.' Guaranteed million-dollar prize, with the house taking no rake. No-limit holdem. Winner take all."

"A genuine freeze-out? No second place?"

"Second place is a signed copy of *Poker for Dummies*."

"What's the buy-in?" he asks.

"Ten large."

He doesn't say anything, and I listen to the wind again.

"Dude, you still breathing?"

"I might be a little short," he says at last.

"That sucks." I felt bad for him, but at the same time I was thinking that if Denn couldn't play, that would make one less top player I'd have to beat.

He says, "Listen, Jimbo, you remember one time you told me about the toughest game in town?"

"Remind me."

"You told me about this little stud game you got in once."

"Oh, yeah." I laugh, remembering. "Lousy Lou's."

"That's it. Lousy Lou's."

"Toughest players I ever had the misfortune to sit down with. What do you want to know that for?"

"You know how they say you can't climb out of a hole till you hit bottom?"

"Yeah?"

"I'm trying to find the bottom."

13

(Cattie)

CATTIE KNEW MOST OF THE JOINTS IN VEGAS, but this was the first time she'd been to King's Crossing. The place looked like a Kmart wrapped in neon. She handed her car keys to the valet.

"When did this place open?" she asked him.

"Just last week," said the valet. "Used to be one of them discount stores."

Inside, the Kmart-turned-casino looked the same as every other Vegas money pit: row after row of slot machines occasionally interrupted by a cluster of blackjack tables, a roulette wheel, or a craps table. There weren't a lot of customers—just enough to keep the slots clanging. Cattie threaded her way through the maze of machines and tables, moving toward the back of the casino. Slots, blackjack, keno, and craps were the big moneymakers. Live poker was stuck way in the back of most casinos.

Cattie expected to find a cramped little card-room, four or five tables, but she was surprised. The King's Crossing poker room was enormous: more than fifty new poker tables in a space large enough to accommodate twice that number.

There were only half a dozen games going. Morty Deasel, wearing a yellow- and black-checked sport coat, was leaning against the front podium.

"Hey, kid."

Cattie gave him a cool look. "The unavoidable Morty Deasel," she said.

Morty laughed. "You here to play, or you looking for 'da man'?"

"I don't gamble, Morty."

"Course you don't." He picked up the phone to call upstairs. Cattie wandered over to one of the games, $15-$30 holdem, and watched a few hands. She recognized a couple of the players, local small-time pros eking out a living, trying to survive on fifteen or twenty bucks an hour profit. The others were tourists giving their money away.

She imagined Denn sitting in a game like that. He would destroy it.

Cattie shook her head. No matter how good he was at poker, Denn Doyle had no place in a world infested with the likes of Morty Deasel and Cattie Hart. He would be eaten alive. She hoped he would go running back to the real world.

Funny thing was, she had actually liked him. She had liked the way he looked at her, and his sense of humor, and the way he kissed.

Yes, the kisses had been good. She hadn't planned to let it go that far, but somehow when she was spending time with him, she had managed to forget that he was just another mark.

Cattie felt a twinge of regret slithering up through her gut. Regret for what? For hurting Denn, or for letting herself care about him? She closed her eyes, cast her regret into a closet, and slammed the door.

Guilt was for suckers.

14

(Denn)

DENN PARKED HIS CAR BENEATH THE flickering light of a dying neon sign that had once read Lou's Lucky Lounge. But half of the neon tubes were broken or burned out, and what remained of the sign now read Lou's—y Lou—.

Lousy Lou's.

Jimbo had told Denn he'd discovered Lousy Lou's by accident: He'd busted a fan belt while driving past the joint, ducked inside to get out of the heat while he waited for the tow truck, and found himself sitting in on a game of seven-card stud.

The toughest game he'd ever seen, Jimbo had said with a grin.

Denn pulled the pathetic roll of ones and fives from the front pocket of his warm-ups.

He counted it again.

Ninety-seven dollars.

Enough? He would soon find out.

Inside, Lousy Lou's was one of those long, dark, smoky beer joints where the only illumination came from a bank of aging slots and a neon beer sign behind the bar. Two shapeless lumps hunched over the bar turned pale faces toward him as he entered; they found little of interest and returned their attention to their drinks. Denn took a few seconds to let his eyes adjust to the gloom, then took a stool at the end of the bar and ordered a beer.

The bartender, a doughy man with sagging jowls and a bloodshot nose, popped open a can of Pepsi and skidded it across the bar.

"Funny-looking beer," Denn said.

"I got grandkids your age," the bartender growled.

Denn heard laughter and the rattle of chips coming from the back room.

"That a poker game I hear back there?"

The bartender nodded. "One-to-four stud. You buy your chips from me. You lose 'em back there."

"Maybe I won't lose."

The bartender shrugged. "Whatever you say, kid."

Denn plonked his money on the bar. "I'll take my chances."

The bartender extracted a rack of one hundred worn, discolored chips from behind the cash register and set it on the bar.

"Don't say I didn't warn you." He counted Denn's money, then removed five chips from the rack.

"Two for the 'beer,'" he said.

Denn figured he'd be the youngest player—he usually was—but what he saw almost made him laugh out loud. It looked like a scene from a rest home for burned-out gamblers: four wrinkly old dudes in various states of decrepitude, all of them wearing glasses thick as Texas toast, and two old ladies—twins, apparently—wearing matching orange wigs.

The dealer, who was relatively young—maybe only sixty—looked up at Denn and said, "Open seat, sir."

Denn set his rack of chips on the table.

Five hundred years' worth of wrinkles turned to look at him.

He could tell from the way they ogled his chips, six pink tongues moistening six sets of withered lips, that the usual buy-in was far less than ninety-five dollars. He hadn't played for stakes this low since Fairview.

One of the players said, "You could just give us

your money right now—save yourself some time."
They all laughed.

Denn laughed too, then sat down.

"Guess he's going to make us earn it, Herman,"
said a guy with an unlit cigar embedded in the corner of his mouth. The cigar looked as if it had been
there for a week.

Inwardly Denn smiled. Jimbo had been pulling
his leg. This game looked about as tough as a bowl
of marshmallow soup. Give him a couple hours and
he'd clean them all out. He almost felt bad about it.
They were probably living on social security, eating
oatmeal three times a day.

Denn put on his sunglasses and plugged in his
iPod and sank into his zone. Several seconds later
he noticed that the other players were staring at
him.

"What?"

"You don't like us, kid?"

"What do you mean?"

"He's hiding," said one of the redheaded twins.
She licked two fingers, reached over, and dragged
her wet fingertips down the lenses of Denn's shades.

"Hey!" Denn snatched the glasses off his face.

"There he is," said the other twin.

Denn stared at the two streaks of old lady spit on
his glasses.

"We don't wear cheaters, kid," explained one of the old men, following that up with a series of rattling coughs that sounded like the last gasps of a dying asthmatic.

Denn looked at the ring of spectacled faces. Their eyeglasses were so thick that they might as well have been sunglasses.

"Whatever," he said.

"Kids say that all the time these days, Herman," said another player, a black guy with a few tufts of white hair still clinging to his head. "Whatever this, whatever that. Like they don't want to make a choice."

"They think the cards will tell them what to do, Moe," said the one with the purple thing growing on the side of his nose. "I used to be like that."

"They don't think at all," said Moe.

"Sorry," said Denn. "I didn't know about the sunglasses rule, okay?"

"Kids," Herman muttered, shaking his head.

Thirty minutes later Denn was down fifty bucks.

The stud players were half in the grave, they were playing for pitifully low stakes, and they were kicking his young ass. They were cagey, cautious, opportunistic, and cheap, tipping the dealer a quarter, if that, and taking liberal advantage of the free coffee offered by the house. Living on social security, Denn figured. Counting every penny.

One of the geezers, the geriatric case they called Flash, turned to him.

"You usually play higher stakes, don't you, son?"

"A little," Denn said.

"I used to do that," Flash said, running a shaking hand over his grizzled chin. "Used to play me a lot of thirty-sixty. Midge and Marge here, they used to play seventy-five–one-fifty lowball over Gardena way."

"Went broke, huh?" Denn said, thinking he was being sympathetic.

"Broke?" Flash scowled at him. "Hell, no. We retired, son. These days we just play to relax."

Denn figured the old dude was full of it.

But he wasn't sure.

He forgot about the low stakes and the fact that he was now playing with his last forty-five bucks, and he focused on the game with the same intensity he would bring to a $400-$800 game. One thing about low-limit stud—the margins were razor thin. No room for mistakes. Losing ten or twelve dollars on a pot was a major setback. And these fossils were making very few mistakes.

Slowly the worm turned. Denn began to pick up a small pot now and then.

He played for another three hours, slowly building his stack a few chips at a time, then losing them back again. He had stopped the bleeding, but he was still down nearly a quarter of his original stack. The stud players began to grumble and fidget once it became clear that Denn was not going to throw his money away anymore, and the game broke up with Denn still down twenty-two dollars.

When he cashed in his remaining chips, the bartender said, "You musta caught some good cards, kid."

15

(Denn)

DENN DROVE BACK TO HIS APARTMENT, thinking back over the game at Lousy Lou's, thinking through each hand, card by card.

The bartender was right. He had caught a few good cards toward the end of the evening. He'd gotten lucky and only lost twenty-two dollars. Denn knew he had played most of the hands okay, but most wasn't good enough. One mistake could wipe out two hours' worth of profits. In a game that tight there was only one option: to play flawlessly.

He should never have slow-played that set of jacks—holdem strategy had no place in a screwed-down, low-limit seven-stud game. And he'd made a huge mistake betting into Moe's pair of eights a few hands later. He should have seen how Midge's smile had faded when Moe caught that second eight.

Reading tells wasn't just about the person whose hand you were trying to read. In a game like Lousy

Lou's, you had to pay attention to how the other players reacted to one another's play. If Midge was worried about Moe's hand, she probably had reason to be. Those six old gamblers knew each other better than Denn ever would.

He let himself into his apartment, flipped on the light, and looked around. His apartment was neat, clean, and utterly without character. No plants, no artwork, no pets, no smells, no nothing. The black-leather sofa set, the stereo, the big-screen TV he never watched—all rented, because he couldn't be bothered to go shopping. A few books, mostly on poker strategy, half filled a rented oak bookshelf. The books, he owned.

He poured himself a glass of grape juice. The only other occupant of his small refrigerator was a jar of dill pickles. He found a box of crackers in one of his many nearly empty cupboards, sat at the kitchenette counter, and made a meal of crackers, pickles, and grape juice.

A pizza would be nice.

He counted his money. His original ninety-seven dollars, minus the twenty-two he'd lost, minus the two bucks he'd spent on "beer." With only seventy-three dollars to his name, he was not about to drop ten bucks on a pizza. If he wanted to eat pizza, he would have to play better poker.

He thought about the tournament Jimbo had mentioned. Winner take all, with a million-dollar-plus payday. A million bucks would put him back in action. The problem was coming up with the $10,000 entry fee.

How long would it take him to win ten grand off the fossil collection at Lousy Lou's?

About twenty years.

Denn stared into his grape juice. What were his chances of turning his seventy-three dollars into ten grand in the next week? Not great. And even if he did come up with it, how stupid would he have to be to invest it all-in in a winner-take-all poker tournament?

Pretty stupid.

He ate the last pickle, but saved a few crackers for breakfast.

Tomorrow was going to be a long, hungry day.

16

(Cattie)

CATTIE FIGURED THE GRAY MAN MIGHT collapse and die at any moment. Or maybe he was a corpse already and just didn't know it.

He sat behind his desk talking on his phone and smoking a cigarette with a long gray ash, looking as if he'd stepped out of a black-and-white movie, his gray eyes staring right through her.

He had found Cattie in Reno, where she had been working with Jerry Burkhardt, the card counter she'd met in Tahoe. Jerry would sit at a blackjack table making minimum bets and counting off the cards in his head. When he found a deck that was rich with aces, faces, and tens, he would signal Cattie to slide into one of the other seats and make the big bets.

It was strictly small time. They didn't have much of a bankroll, and every time they got a few bucks ahead, Jerry would bet it on a football game.

Jerry was not a lucky man.

Also, he was a lousy counter.

But they made enough to pay for their hotel rooms, food, and other expenses. At one point Jerry suggested that they save money by sharing a hotel room. Cattie laughed at him, and he dropped the subject, but she knew it would come up again.

They had been working the tables at Harrah's one night. Jerry kept screwing up the count, going through their money at five bucks a hand, every now and then shooting her this hangdog look. Cattie, forty feet away, was playing the nickel slots and waiting for him to give her the high sign, when she felt a presence to her left. She turned her head and found herself staring into the flattest, deadest, grayest pair of eyes she had ever seen.

"You could do better," the man said.

Cattie gave him her phoniest smile. "You've got a better chance with Marilyn Monroe, old man." She said. "Go dig her up." She returned her attention to Jerry and the slot machine.

After a couple of minutes, during which Jerry lost four more hands and Cattie lost twenty-four nickels, the man, still standing there, said, "The red hair is nice. Is it real?"

Cattie gave him her hard-eyed look. "Your skin looks like you died in it. Is it real?"

"Ha. Ha. Ha." He lit a cigarette. "It's a condition." He inhaled deeply, then said, "Would you
like to make some real money?"

"I'm doing fine."

"Security is about to drop the hammer on you
and your boyfriend."

"He's not my boyfriend."

"Then what's your problem?"

Cattie looked back at Jerry. Three large men
wearing dark suits and grim expressions were standing close behind him. One of them reached out and
put a plate-size hand on Jerry's shoulder.

She stood up and said to the gray man, "Tell me
more."

A few days later he moved her to Vegas and got
her a job dealing poker at the Sand Dunes, where
after a few weeks he pointed out a tall, dark-haired
young man playing in a holdem tournament.

"You see that kid?"

"That's him?" Cattie asked.

"That's him. Do you think you can fall in love
with him?"

Cattie laughed. "He's kind of cute."

Ashtray-scented air hissed from the gray man's
nose.

Cattie said, "He'll either like me or he won't."

"He will like you, Catherine."

He was right. She and Denn had gotten along just fine.

.

Cattie squirmed in her chair, wishing he would get on with it. She'd been watching the Corpse—that was her new name for him, she decided—watching him talk on the phone for ten minutes. She stood up and walked to the window and looked out over the four-acre parking lot. Judging from the number of empty spaces, King's Crossing was not doing much business.

She heard him hang up the phone.

"Do you like the view?"

"Nothing like a big empty parking lot."

"You young people are so blasé."

"Whatever. You said you had a job for me."

He walked around his desk and stood beside her at the window. "This parking lot will not be empty for long. I have big plans for King's Crossing. The publicity for my poker tournament will bring us a lot of new business, and that is only the beginning."

"I'm happy for you."

"Ha. Ha. Ha. It won't be easy, Catherine. I am going to need your help."

"What do you want me to do?"

His arm slithered across her back; his cool hand cupped her shoulder. He said, "I want you to become my personal assistant."

17

(Denn)

"OPEN SEAT, KID," SAID MOE.

Denn set his rack containing seventy-three dollars in chips on the edge of the table.

The same six geriatric cases—Herman, Moe, Flash, Walt, Midge, and Marge—sitting around the same table playing the same game, $1-$4 stud. Ten o'clock in the morning and it was as if they had never left.

Denn sat between Midge and Marge, the twin redheads.

"You're cute," said Midge, adjusting her wig.

"Thanks," said Denn.

"You look familiar," said Herman, staring at him through thick, greasy eyeglasses with plastic frames that might have been in fashion back in 1978.

"I was here yesterday," Denn said. "Taking lessons."

"Oh, yeah, I remember you."

They all laughed. Anything any of them said about memory or remembering was considered funny.

"I remember you, too," said Flash, the oldest and slowest of them all.

They all laughed again.

"Ante up, kids," said the dealer.

After half an hour Denn was up seven dollars and twenty-five cents. Not bad. He had recouped one third of yesterday's losses. Another seven hundred hours and he'd have his buy-in for that tournament.

Moe said, "What are you doing here anyways, kid?" He bet two dollars on fifth street with an ace, king, nine showing.

"Gambling," Denn said, folding his pair of jacks.

"You call that gambling?" Moe showed his hole cards—pocket tens—as the dealer pushed him the pot. "I bet you folded the best hand, kid."

Denn smiled. "That's a good bet." He would remember that. And he would remember the fact that Moe wanted him to remember it.

"You got to know when to hold 'em," Herman gurgled in his phlegmy voice.

"Know when to fold 'em," Flash sang creakily.

Midge and Marge tittered as Herman erupted into another series of death rattles.

Denn kept the smile on his face, but he was thinking, *If I can't beat this game, I'm giving up poker for good.*

Moe said, "I was your age, kid, I was out chasin' girls, not playing poker with a bunch of fossils. Don't you like girls?"

"I like some of them," said Denn, thinking of Cattie for the first time since he had sat down.

Something must have shown on his face, because Marge leaned into him and spoke in a low voice. "Do you have a broken heart, child?"

Denn forced out a laugh, shaking his head.

Moe said, "I bet he's one of them homosexuals."

Marge smiled sweetly and said to Moe, "Let him be, Moses. Can't you see he has a broken heart?"

18

(Denn)

BY HIS FOURTH DAY AT LOUSY LOU'S, DENN
had learned a few things. Moe had a slight tendency
to overplay his cards late in the hand. Midge was a
little gun-shy on her draws. Flash played an utterly
disciplined and unimaginative game, which made
him easy to read but tough to extract money from.
Herman and Walt played nearly as tight as Flash,
but both had tells: Herman let his shoulders drop a
scant centimeter when he had a made hand, while
Walt tended to push his chips out a little more force-
fully when he was playing a draw.

Marge turned out to be the toughest of the
bunch, changing speeds on nearly every hand, and
every tell Denn thought he identified in her turned
out to be a red herring. But he learned to keep an eye
on her twin sister, Midge, when Marge was in a
hand. Midge got this faint smile when she knew her
sister was snowing, but went blank-faced when

Marge held a big hand. As long as Midge could read Marge, Denn didn't need to.

Denn had them figured out, but that didn't make it easy. They still played nearly perfectly. He was picking up a few pots—his bankroll was up to $124—but extracting money from that bunch was like squeezing blood from a stone.

That was, until he hit his heater.

19

(Jimbo)

SOONER OR LATER, EVERY POKER PLAYER GOES on a rush. The odds seem to go whacko, and suddenly you can do no wrong. You get dealt pocket sixes and fill up on the river to beat an ace-high flush. You call with deuces and it turns out your opponent was bluffing with a busted flush. You flop sets, turn boats, river quads, fill your gut shots, and your wired aces hold up every time. I once saw a guy in a full holdem game win twelve pots running. They had to stop the game to give him time to stack all his chips.

Anyway, that's how it went for Denn that day at Lousy Lou's. He hit a heater to end all heaters, and by the time the game broke up he had won himself more than $400. That might not seem like a lot of money, and it's not, but if you knew how tight that game was, you might sooner believe in leprechauns and Santa Claus.

Fact is, I *didn't* believe it when I heard, so I stop in at Lousy Lou's. Mack, the dealer, is sitting at the bar nursing a beer. I ask him what really happened and he tells me it went down just like I heard.

"That damned kid destroyed my game," Mack says. "I haven't seen Moe, Flash, or Walt since. The twins stopped in, but they didn't want to play heads-up with just each other. They told me Herman's in the hospital now with angina or something."

"What are you gonna do?" I ask him.

Mack shrugs. "I hear they're hiring dealers at that new joint, King's Crossing."

Of course, I'm wondering what the kid is going to do with the four hundred he had won.

I don't have to wonder for long.

That same day I'm stuck a thousand bucks playing $30-$60 at the Bellagio and I see the kid's black mop sticking up out of the $6-$12 game a few tables over, so I take a break and go over to watch a few hands.

One thing I notice right away: The kid is still wearing that black and blue track suit, but no shades and no iPod. Weird to see his eyes, brown so dark you can't hardly make out his pupils, moving in little jerks as he follows the action. I try to think if I've ever seen him without those shades on.

It don't take a genius to see why the kid is so good. Most players, when they aren't in a hand, will talk, or count their chips, or look around for a pretty girl to rest their eyes on, or do something else to keep themselves amused.

Not Denn.

When he is out of a hand he watches the other players.

"Dude," I say. "Swimming with the minnows again?"

Denn mucks his hand but keeps his eyes on the action. "I liked that game, Jimbo."

"Lousy Lou's?"

He nods.

"I hear you destroyed it," I say.

"I got lucky."

He looks at the new cards that have been dealt him. Pocket tens. The player under the gun raises, the next player reraises. Denn mucks his tens and riffles a stack of chips, ignoring me, intently watching the players who were still in the hand.

"I saw her," I say.

His head jerks up, and he looks at me.

"King's Crossing," I say. "I think maybe she's working there."

The kid nods slowly. "Thanks." He returns his focus to the game and doesn't look at me again.

20

(Denn)

AFTER FOUR DAYS OF PLAYING AT LOUSY Lou's, sitting at that $6-$12 table at the Bellagio was like playing with children. The other players were tourists, drinking and throwing their money around and doing their best to have a good time in Vegas before crawling back to Muncie or Minneapolis or Memphis or wherever. Three hours into the game he was up $230.

He looked across the room to the glassed-in high-stakes section, where Jen, Sammy, Brunson, Chip Reese, and the other high-stakes players would be betting more on each hand than the sum of all the chips at this crappy little $6-$12 table.

A week ago he had been one of the elite. Now he was reduced to bottom-feeding at the tourist tables.

And Cattie Hart was working at King's Crossing.

He shook his head, throwing off the thought. He

could not afford to lose focus. One twelve-dollar bet meant more to him now than a thousand dollars had meant a week ago.

Focus. That was why he'd left his iPod and shades at home. He would not allow himself to go on automatic, not even for one hand. He had learned that at Lousy Lou's. Every bet counted.

New hand. The Hispanic woman to his left looked at her cards and her hand twitched, an involuntary grab for her chips. The skinny guy to his right called the blind. Denn checked his own hand. Ace, ten. Into the muck. The woman to his left raised, as he knew she would.

Thoughts of Cattie fluttered at the periphery of his thoughts like moths beating their wings on a window. Now that he knew where she was working, he knew he would have to go see her. But he would not let her interfere with his play in the here and now. He thrust her away, keeping his head in the game.

The Hispanic woman took down the pot with pocket kings. The dealer shuffled and fired out another round of cards. Denn did not look at his cards—he kept his attention on the other players. The guy with the shades folded. A soft-faced man wearing a Minnesota Twins cap raised, pushing out two neat stacks of chips, saying nothing. The last time he had bet like that, quiet and neat, he'd had pocket queens.

Now Denn looked at his cards. King, jack. He folded. Two other players called.

The dealer flopped an ace, jack, trey.

The guy in the Twins cap bet out. Denn figured him for a big pair, but not aces, or he would have sandbagged. Denn's king, jack might have been good, but he didn't regret folding—not for a moment. The player two seats to his left, a burly young man wearing a University of Arizona sweatshirt, raised. The next player, a jittery woman wearing too much makeup, called. The Twins cap guy called as well.

The turn brought a queen. The Twins cap guy scowled, shrugged, and checked. The act was so transparent that Denn could hardly believe the other players didn't see it. Clearly, the guy had pocket queens.

Oblivious, the burly guy bet and the jittery woman called.

The Twins cap guy raised.

The burly guy—Denn now put him on an ace, jack—reraised. The woman, realizing that she was getting whipsawed, folded. The Twins cap guy raised again, and this time the burly guy had the sense to just call.

A deuce came on the river, helping neither player. The Twins cap guy collected one more bet and took the pot down with his set of queens. The burly guy showed his ace, jack, and Denn congratulated himself on a perfect read.

And so it went. Several hours later, with his stack up to $1000, Denn felt himself losing focus. Thoughts of Cattie kept coming at him. He thought about going to King's Crossing to look her up.

Two new cards appeared before him. Pocket tens. He raised and got called by the guy on the button. The flop came eight, seven, three. Denn bet out. The guy on the button raised. Denn kicked him back. The button reraised. Denn looked at him—a flat-faced, middle-aged guy wearing a rumpled sport coat—and realized that he had no read on the guy at all. In fact, he hadn't even noticed when he had joined the game.

"Where did you come from?" Denn asked.

The guy gave him a puzzled look. "I been here half an hour, sport."

Denn called the raise.

The turn was an ace. Denn bet, just to see if his jacks were good. The flat-faced guy raised.

Realizing he was lost in the hand, Denn mucked his cards, racked his chips, cashed in, and left.

You got to know when to hold 'em, and you got to know when to fold 'em, but most important of all, you got to know when to get the hell out of Dodge.

21

(Cattie)

IF THERE WAS ONE THING CATTIE HAD learned from her mother, Heather, it was that money was the key to happiness, but no matter how much of it you had, that door never seemed to open. One of her earliest memories was of her mother screaming at her dad about money. By the time Cattie entered the first grade, her mother had screamed him right out of their double-wide mobile home and out of their lives.

"Good riddance," Heather had said.

Cattie hadn't seen her father since.

That was something she had in common with Denn. Both of their dads had left. Denn's dad, at least, still gave his mom money. Cattie's mom had had to go out and get it on her own.

Heather Hart had tried working as a hairdresser. She had sold Avon products. She had cashiered for a while at the Wal-Mart. She had tried selling magazine subscriptions by phone. She worked hard at everything she did, but none of it paid very well.

There was never enough money.

Heather's dream was to win the lottery. No matter how broke they were, she always bought lottery tickets every night. Once, she won $1000 on a scratch-off ticket. They went out to dinner and a movie, then to the Wal-Mart. They bought a new TV, and Cattie got a pink bicycle, and her mom bought herself two new outfits. She spent the remaining $200 on a long strip of scratch-off tickets from the Quik Mart.

None of the tickets paid off more than a dollar or two. A few days later Cattie's new bike was stolen, and everything went back to the way it was before, except that they had a better TV.

Finally—Cattie must have been about ten, old enough to babysit herself—her mother took a job as a cocktail waitress at the Grey Goose Lounge.

Heather could be an attractive woman when she made the effort, and she began to bring home a series of boyfriends—as many as three or four a week—mostly men she met at the Grey Goose. These boyfriends, it turned out, could also be a source of jewelry, money, and other gifts.

Some nights she didn't come home at all.

Cattie did not like to think about those years.

She didn't know which was worse, the nights of listening to the voices of strange men, and the noises they would make, or the nights when she was alone in the mobile home, lying awake listening to the creaks and pops and scratching noises. By the time she was thirteen, she was spending nearly all her time in her tiny bedroom at the back of the double-wide, making occasional runs to the kitchen or bathroom, but mostly staying in her room to avoid her mother—and her mother's boyfriends.

They had more money then, but it was still never enough, and somehow it was always a crisis when it came time to make the monthly payment on the double-wide.

Often, in the morning, to avoid listening to her mother's hungover bitching about her latest guy, Cattie would walk to the Church of the Sacred Heart and sit at the back and listen to the dried-out old priest deliver his daily mass to a bunch of old ladies all clustered in the front three rows of pews. Her favorite part was the sermon, which usually began with a short passage from the Bible, then morphed into a strident rant about the evils of fornication, abortion, tobacco, liquor, rock-and-roll, and immodest apparel. Cattie admired the old priest for his passion and certainty, even though she thought it was all a bunch of crap.

School provided no refuge. Cattie had little interest in academics, and she had no friends. The other students ignored her, with the exception of the occasional cruel remark, such as the time Ginger Thule walked up to her in the hall with a big fake-friendly smile and said, "Hey, Cattie, is it true that your mom's a slut?"

Cattie did not hesitate for one second. She hit Ginger so hard that the girl's lower lip split wide open, spilling blood down over her chin.

Ginger needed several stitches. Cattie was kicked out of school.

It was around then that Cattie dyed her hair and entered her everything-black phase.

Of course, Cattie knew that Ginger was right. Her mother could dress it up however she liked. She could call her male friends "boyfriends," and she could call the things they left behind "presents," but even at thirteen Cattie knew that her mom was nothing but a trailer-park whore.

"Catherine?"

Cattie blinked back the memories and looked at the gray man sitting across from her. It was late, and there were only a few people still in the restaurant.

"Sorry. Did you say something?"

"I said you look lovely tonight."

"Thank you."

The funny thing about money, Cattie thought, was that unlike her mother Cattie had never had any problem hanging on to it. She had $60,000 in a safe-deposit box at Bank One and $10,000 holding up the short leg of her kitchen table at home, and now the Corpse wanted to put her on his payroll at $2000 a week. No, getting money wasn't her problem. Cattie's problem was that spending it brought her no pleasure.

Not that she hadn't tried. She had bought herself clothes, and jewelry, and a car, and expensive meals. But every time she made a big purchase, she only felt worse. She felt—there was no other word for it—guilty. Maybe all those ridiculous sermons she'd listened to at Sacred Heart had poisoned her mind.

Cattie picked up her fork and poked listlessly at her chocolate torte. She had only been able to eat one bite, and she knew she could not possibly swallow another.

It was delicious.

22

(Denn)

STANDING BENEATH THE ARCHWAY AT THE entrance to the King's Crossing poker room, Denn scanned the room for Cattie. The only redhead he could see was a forty-something plus-size in a green dress. Not even close.

Denn was surprised by the size of the room. He counted the tables. Fifty-two. One table for each card in the deck. Did that make it the biggest card-room in Vegas? He thought so.

At the moment, only seven tables were active.

To his left was a poster advertising the Big Deal. Ten grand to enter, winner take all. He wondered how many players would sign up. Would it be like the World Series of Poker, with thousands of entrants? Denn didn't think so. The WSOP's $10,000 main event awarded prizes to several dozen people, spreading the wealth. The Big Deal, with only one winner, would not attract as many players.

Denn walked over to the board, where a bored-looking white-haired man was leaning against a podium. He saw Denn coming and perked up.

"Care to play some poker, sir?" The man's name badge read HARLEY.

"Cattie here?" Denn asked.

Harley frowned. "Cathy?"

"Cattie. Cattie Hart. I think she works here as a dealer."

"Sorry."

"A redhead? About so high. Nice-looking?"

Harley shook his head. "We've hired a lot of new dealers this week, getting ready for the Big Deal."

"How many people have signed up so far?" Denn asked.

"Fifty-seven," said Harley.

"How many are you expecting?"

The man shrugged. "No idea. It's a freeze-out, you know. Only one winner. And we're not running any satellites. You have to come up with the ten K to enter. That scares a lot of them off. Why, you interested?"

"Maybe later," Denn said. He looked at the board listing the active games. Might as well sit in on a game while he was here. "Got a fifteen-thirty holdem seat?"

"Yes, sir, I certainly do," said Harley.

Sixty seconds later Denn was stacking his chips, watching the cards, the hands, the faces.

23

(Cattie)

BEING THE CORPSE'S PERSONAL ASSISTANT didn't come with a job description, but Cattie thought she knew what he wanted from her.

He wasn't going to get it.

Maybe she would tell him she had AIDS.

She looked over at him, his manicured, gray hands on the steering wheel, guiding his Lincoln Navigator up Las Vegas Boulevard, so smooth and quiet that the casinos drifting past looked like images on a movie screen.

"I'd like to show you my house," he said.

"I'd love to see it," Cattie said. "Maybe another time."

"Have you ever swum in an infinity pool?"

Cattie had seen pictures. An infinity pool had one side that just . . . ended. Like the end of the world. Water went right up to the edge and fell away.

"No," she said. "And no, thank you. I'm feeling a little sick. I think I ate too much."

"You hardly ate a thing."

"Like I said, I'm feeling not so good. Can you just drop me off at my car?"

He gave her a flat, measuring look. Cattie returned it, refusing to back down.

"Nothing is free," he said.

"You want me to pay my share of the dinner?"

He shook his head slowly, his lips turning up into a cold smile.

Cattie thought back to the incompetent Jerry Burkhardt counting cards in Reno. Maybe she would have been better off staying with him. At least she had been able to control Jerry. This guy she wasn't so sure about.

His cell phone went off. He plugged his earpiece in and said, "What."

He listened, blinking, guiding the SUV in and out of traffic.

"I'll be there in a few minutes."

Cattie felt herself relax. If he had some business to take care of, he might forget about her, at least for the night.

Five minutes later they pulled up in front of King's Crossing.

"Keep it parked right here," he said to the valet.

Cattie started toward the side lot, where she had left her car.

"Catherine!" His voice struck her like a whip.

She stopped.

"Join me for a drink, would you please?"

Cattie shrugged and went to him. He wrapped an arm around her shoulders.

"Cold," he said.

"It's ninety degrees out here."

"That's not what I meant."

Together, they entered the casino.

24

(Denn)

IT WAS A SOFT GAME. DENN DIDN'T KNOW ANY of the other players, but he figured them out fast. Tourists. A fold-and-wait game. No point in making fancy plays. No point in bluffing. Just sit and fold hand after hand, waiting for two good cards—ace, king or a big pocket pair—then bet 'em.

Boring, but profitable.

Denn slowly gathered chips. In the first hour he won $270. Halfway through the second hour he was up another ninety when he felt a shiver travel up his spine. He looked up and caught a glimpse of red hair on the other side of the room.

He folded his hand—an ace, jack offsuit—and craned his neck for a better look, but a small crowd of railbirds watching the action at a $5-$10 table blocked his view.

Denn pushed back his chair and stood up.

There. He saw the back of her head disappearing into the lounge.

Leaving his chips on the table, he walked quickly toward the lounge, silently rehearsing his one and only question: *Why?*

The lounge was dim compared with the brightly lit cardroom. Several small round tables were scattered in front of a gleaming chromium and red vinyl bar. The bartender was pouring champagne into two tall flutes. Cattie was sitting at one of the tables along the wall, facing him. A gray-haired man in a suit sat across from her, smoking a long cigarette.

Cattie's eyes found Denn. Their eyes locked.

Denn walked up to the table.

"Hey," said Cattie.

The man in the suit turned and looked up.

Denn felt his heart stop. It felt like several seconds, but it could not have been that long. He just had time to wonder if he was about to die; then his heart started up again.

Thump.

"Hey, kid," said the man.

Denn nodded, wearing his poker face. Inside his head, the cards were shuffling in reverse, all the suits and ranks falling into place. Everything was starting to make sense.

"Artie," he said.

25

(Cattie)

"SIDDOWN, KID," ARTIE KINGSTON SAID, gesturing with his cigarette. "Take a load off."

Denn didn't move for a few seconds. Then he pulled a chair over to the table and sat down, Cattie on his left, Artie on his right. He kept his eyes on Artie.

Cattie sat back in her chair and watched them both. She did not like what she was feeling.

Artie said, "So how are you doing, kid? I hear you had a rough couple weeks."

"I've had better," said Denn. "How about you? I haven't seen you since I won that restaurant off you back in Fairview."

"I'm doing okay." Artie gestured to include their surroundings. "My new venture." He inhaled through his cigarette.

"Nice," said Denn. "Kind of like a Kmart with slots."

Artie laughed, "Ha. Ha. Ha," sending out a puff of smoke with each "ha."

Denn turned to Cattie. "Does he pay you well?"

"I pay her extremely well," said Artie.

Cattie started to stand up. Artie's hand shot across the table and grabbed her arm. She froze, halfway to standing.

"Stay, Catherine."

Cattie used her free hand to peel his fingers from her arm. It was like unbending cold, dry sausages.

He withdrew his hand. "Catherine . . ."

She grabbed her purse and walked quickly out of the bar, through the casino, and out into the bright Las Vegas night.

26

(Denn)

"SHE LIKES YOU," SAID ARTIE.

"Really," said Denn. This was not a dream. But it sure felt like one. Artie Kingston looked even worse than he had back in Fairview—like a corpse from a zombie movie, no more real than the figures at Madame Tussaud's wax museum. "She likes me so much she dropped a deck on me."

Artie produced a sandpaper-on-stone chuckle.

"She really does like you, kid. Know how I can tell?"

Denn shook his head.

"Because when I told her she was going to take you for everything you had, she asked me why."

"What did you tell her? That it was because I busted your ass?"

"No. I told her it was a matter of principle. In any case, I got that restaurant back for a song. Tony

Sicard is still back in Fairview running the joint for me. He got the liquor license reinstated. Even has a little holdem game going most nights in the back room. Hundred-dollar buy-in. Even a drag-ass loser like you could afford it."

It made sense. A guy like Artie Kingston would never walk away from a tough beat without plotting to reverse his losses. He had probably instructed Sicard to see that the restaurant failed under Denn's ownership so he could buy it back cheap.

"You know, kid, you never had a chance. Not really. This game is not just about luck and talent."

"What game is that?" Denn asked, even though he thought he knew.

"This game." Artie spread his arms to include the entire universe. "You know what this game is about?"

"I have a feeling you're about to tell me."

Artie's mouth curved into a cold smile. "It's about making people do what you want. I'm sorry to tell you, kid, but you come up short."

"Gee, thanks, Artie. Any other good news?"

"How's your bankroll looking, kid?"

Denn was not about to tell Artie Kingston anything about his bankroll. "Why should that matter to you?"

"I was wondering if you'd be playing in the Big Deal."

"I haven't decided," Denn said. The fact was, he was almost nine grand short of the buy-in.

"You don't want to take another shot at me?"

"You're playing in your own tournament?"

Artie shrugged. "Why not? It's my tournament."

"Tell me something," Denn said. "How did you arrange for me to lose six nights in a row at the Bellagio?"

Artie coughed up a wheezy chuckle.

"Kid, you're easy as a ten-dollar hooker. Your game is all about reads, right? You put the other player on a hand and you play him like you know what he's got. You read tells like a road map. And you're good at it, I'll give you that. But a guy who depends on tells is a guy with his head on the block. Especially if he's stupid enough to share what he knows with his sweetie."

Inside, Denn's organs seemed to be rearranging themselves. If Artie was trying to make him feel like a world class schmuck, he was doing a good job. Denn had told Cattie about the tells he had on Sammy Gold and the other players. She must have told Artie Kingston, who had then informed the players of Denn's reads on them.

Denn felt his face turning red as he thought back over those losing nights at the Bellagio. They must have been laughing at him the whole time, sending him false tells and letting him bet into the nuts, or making him fold the best hand. No wonder he'd lost.

Denn stood up.

"The other factor," Artie said, "is that you were all mush-brained over a piece of tail. You can't fall in love and play poker, kid. They're incompatible."

Denn started to walk away, then turned and asked, "So why didn't you just let the guys at the Bellagio finish me off? For that matter, how come you didn't just sit in on that game and finish me off yourself? Why set me up with Morty and Frisk? Why use Cattie?"

"I was making a point, kid." Artie blew out a long stream of blue smoke and stubbed out his cigarette. "You're just a detail. As for that little redhead—I just threw her in for laughs. I thought you might like to see who your friends aren't."

27

(Jimbo)

IN THE WORLD OF POKER, YOU GOT TO BE careful picking your friends. Because no matter who you hook up with, sooner or later they are going to hit you up for a loan.

Don't get me wrong—I am not averse to fronting a guy a few bucks if I think he's good for it. I once gave my man Derek Wiles five hundred bucks so he could make his rent. I got that back in a week. And plenty of times I've staked guys in games for a piece of the action, like the time I bought Jerry G. into a holdem tournament for $400 and got paid off big when he took second place. Of course, I've lent out lots of twenties and like that, mostly saying bye-bye to the money.

It's all part of the game, part of what you call your gambling economy.

So I'm sitting in a sweet touristy sort of game at

the Mirage, a little after midnight, when I feel Denn ease up behind me. He waits till the hand is over— I win—before he opens his mouth.

"Nice hand," he says. I can tell from his voice that he wants something.

"Thanks." I look at his face for the first time. "You look like hell, dude. When's the last time you slept?"

"You got a minute?"

"Sure." I motion to the dealer to deal me out. "Let's go look at the tigers."

If you haven't seen Siegfried and Roy's white tigers, you really should. Next to the poker action, they're the best thing about the Mirage. Denn and I make small talk on the way to the tiger exhibit, then stand for a while in silence and watch the beasts pacing behind the glass.

"Makes you feel mortal, don't it," I say.

"I saw her," Denn says. "At King's Crossing, like you said."

"You talk to her?"

"She was with somebody."

I wait for more.

"She was with Artie Kingston," he says.

For a second I can't place the name. Then I remember.

"Dude! The guy you won the restaurant from back in Bumfunk?"

"Fairview. But, yeah, that's the guy. He owns King's Crossing."

I think about that, taking in all the implications.

"He a suit? Kind of old and gray, like?"

"That's him."

"I saw him that day you got reamed at the Dunes. Didn't know who he was."

"He set that up."

"That's cold."

"Jimbo, I need a favor."

"Uh-oh. You're gonna ask me for money, aren't you."

"Uh . . . yeah, I am."

"I thought you were doing good. Man, you were up like a thousand bucks last night."

"I'm up about sixteen hundred now, but I need another nine large. I want to enter that tournament."

"The Big Deal? Dude, that's a freeze-out. Odds are you won't cash."

"I'll pay you back, win or lose, and give you twenty percent of my action if I win."

It's a good offer—if he is able to pay me back. But that is no sure thing.

I say, "I'd love to help you, man, but I'm entered in the thing too. You're just one more guy I'd have to beat."

"We swap action. Twenty-five percent. One of us

wins, we pay the other guy a quarter of the net. And I still pay you back plus twenty no matter how it comes down."

I shake my head. "No can do, dude. I'm a little short."

He stares at me, knowing I'm lying. I look away and find myself staring straight into the pale blue eyes of a white tiger.

After a few awkward seconds he says, "Thanks anyway, Jimbo."

I still can't look at him. A few seconds later he walks away, leaving me in my stare-down with the tiger.

The thing is—the thing you got to understand—is that loaning money is like making a bet. You got to look at the odds. And the odds of the kid making good—never mind his little wins over the past few days—were just not that great. The way I saw it, he was still way too messed up over Cattie to keep his head in the game for long. Also, he looked like hell. Like he'd had the life sucked right out of him.

I just couldn't fade that action, Jackson.

28

(Cattie)

CATTIE HAD BEEN THINKING A LOT ABOUT HER mother. A guy with money like Artie Kingston? Heather would have been all over him.

Did the men at the Grey Goose still find her attractive? Did she still bleach her hair and wear those tops so tight it looked like her boobs were about to explode?

Did she ever think about her daughter?

Curled up on her sofa, Cattie hugged herself.

There were moments when she was tempted to pick up the phone and call. It had been six months. Last time she'd tried, Heather had been entertaining a "friend" and had told Cattie she would call her back later.

She never had. A few days later, worried that something had happened, Cattie had tried calling again. Heather had answered the phone with a cheerful hello.

Cattie had hung up.

She wondered what it would feel like if one day she called her mom and the number was disconnected. How would she feel if Heather died? Would she feel anything at all?

Cattie lifted the phone from its base on the end table and held it against her breast. In her mind she went through the motions of punching in the number, silently rehearsing the things she wanted to say. *Are you alive? Are you happy? Do you love me?* All the while knowing she would not make the call.

She let her eyes explore her rented furniture, the cheap artwork that had come with the apartment, the magazines—dozens of them—piled on the coffee table. From her perch on the sofa she could see into the kitchenette. She could see the wad of hundred-dollar bills propping up the short leg of the little table. Maybe she should put them in an envelope and send them to her mom. She twisted her mouth into a grim smile. The money would be gone in a week or two, spent on lottery tickets and booze and God knew what else.

Better to blow the money on herself. Replace some of this crappy furniture. Or buy an expensive watch. Or put it all on a roulette number. Or just give it to one of the panhandlers down on Fremont Street.

She imagined slapping ten grand into some derelict's filthy paw. The astonished look in his eyes. How long would it take him to lose it? Less time than it would take her mother. Less time than it had taken Denn.

Cattie wondered how he was doing. Denn. She wondered if he would go back home to Fairview. She hoped so.

It had been a dangerous pairing, her and Denn. He was lucky. All he had lost was money. He could have done worse.

He could have ended up with her.

Cattie wouldn't wish that fate on anybody. Except maybe Artie.

She closed her eyes and let the phone fall to her lap. It was all so pointless. Sooner or later—probably sooner—Artie would call and ask her to do something.

She would probably do it.

29

(Denn)

DENN WANDERED THROUGH THE MIRAGE, down the rows of slot machines and past the craps tables and roulette wheels, surrounded by hundreds of gamblers but feeling utterly alone.

It had never before bothered him to be alone. In fact, he mostly liked it. He liked seeing himself as the center of a great web, people radiating out from him like drops of dew, each of them connected by a thin, silken strand that he could tug on, or break, at will.

When he was playing cards, that was just how he felt.

With Cattie it had been different. He had felt as if she were a part of him. But seeing her with Artie Kingston had destroyed that, as if a chunk of his soul had torn itself free.

It would hurt for a while yet, but eventually he would think of her no more often than he thought of Kelly Rollingate.

His hand drifted up to touch the chain of gold beads around his neck, the necklace he had bought for Kelly, the gift Kelly had rejected just before dumping him—but the necklace was gone, of course. The last he had seen it was the night it had disappeared into Cattie's purse.

He wished he still had it. He could have pawned it for five or six hundred bucks—which would still leave him eight grand short of the ten he needed for the tournament.

He hadn't been surprised when Jimbo Cowles turned him down, but it had stung. Jimbo was his only friend in Vegas. Hell, anywhere.

Alone. He had always been alone, even when he had thought he wasn't. Even his closest times with Cattie: He had been falling in love with her, and all that time she had been laughing at him.

He stopped and watched a beefy, red-faced man wearing shorts, sandals, and a seersucker sport coat playing blackjack. The man was perspiring heavily, betting $100 a hand and losing. Denn could feel his desperation; he could see it in the man's eyes; he could smell it in his sweat. The guy would just keep playing until he was broke.

Denn turned away. He had seen thousands of compulsive gamblers, but the sight still made him feel slightly ill, as if the man were covered with oozing sores.

Denn did not think of himself as a gambler. Gambling was for losers.

Denn was an investor. When he bet $100 on a pair of jacks, he expected over time to get his hundred back and then some. It was no different from investing in a business, or buying a movie ticket, or getting on an airplane. There was an element of risk, certainly—the business might fail; the movie might suck; the airplane might fall from the sky. But that wasn't really gambling. Not like betting on a hand of blackjack or the spin of a roulette wheel.

Denn looked again at the beefy man and tried to imagine himself pumping out bet after bet, hoping to beat the odds. What was the man feeling? There was desperation, yes, but also a kind of wild joy. Even as the man lost bet after bet, he exuded a sense of repressed triumph. Triumph at stepping into the abyss, at turning himself over to fate, at letting go— something Denn had never been able to do.

What would it feel like?

He felt an impulse to get in his car and drive back to Hoover Dam. Drive right through the guardrail and over the precipice into space. Sink to the bottom of the river and be done with it.

Denn blinked and turned away, shocked by his own thoughts. He had never thought of suicide before, not even for a moment.

What was wrong with him?

Maybe he was just tired. When was the last time he had slept? It was several hours ago that he had left the game at the Bellagio, intending to go back to his apartment to sleep. What time of day had that been? He shook his head to clear it. In Las Vegas nights and days became confused. Inside the casinos there were no windows and no clocks. Time was defined by the relentless clatter of chips and the ringing of the slots and the rise and fall of one's bankroll.

He really should get some sleep.

But tomorrow . . . the tournament was tomorrow. Reaching into his pocket, he felt the roll of bills he had accumulated—one thousand six hundred dollars. If he slept now, he would wake up with only a few hours to turn that money into ten grand. Maybe he should go back into the Bellagio and find a good game and start winning some money.

No. He had left the game there hours ago because he'd been too tired to play well, and then he'd gone to King's Crossing and played some more, and now—he had no idea how many hours later—his eyeballs felt like fried eggs.

The guy at the blackjack table bet his last $100 chip. His face had gone from red to gray; a droplet of sweat jiggled at the end of his nose. Denn watched the cards fall.

The man won. In an instant his expression went from desolate to elated. He bet the whole $200 on the next hand.

He won again.

Five hands later, doubling his stack each time, he was up $3200. He wanted to bet it all. A small crowd had gathered. The dealer called over a pit boss, who approved the bet.

The man won the next four hands, doubling up each time. He had won more than $50,000. He looked like the happiest man on earth.

Denn felt the roll of cash in his front pocket. If he won three hands of blackjack, betting it all each time, he would have $3,200, then $6,400, then $12,800.

Three hands. The odds were against him, but in his mind he could see it happen. People won three hands in a row every day. Every hour. In Vegas it happened every minute. He felt something tense and brittle snap inside his chest, the thing that had always prevented him from taking the worst of it on a bet.

Denn stepped up to the table and laid down his wad of cash.

He felt free, at the mercy of the deck, the same giddy sensation of fear, hope, and letting go that a surgery patient feels as the anesthetic takes hold.

"Welcome to the table, sir," said the dealer.

30

(Cattie)

THE PHONE WOKE HER UP. CATTIE OPENED HER
eyes and turned her head to stare at it.

On the fifth ring her machine answered.

"Catherine."

Cattie didn't move. Sunlight was coming in
around the blinds, making bright stripes on the far
wall.

"I know you're there, Catherine. Why did you
leave last night? It was . . . interesting."

"I bet it was," Cattie said to the answering
machine.

"Your friend is a remarkable young man. Do you
know he still thinks he can beat me? Pick up the
phone, Catherine."

"Screw you, Artie."

"Call me, Catherine. I need you." She heard him
cough, then disconnect.

• • •

Two hours later she called him.

"I'm not interested in your infinity pool," she said.

"Ha. Ha. Ha."

"What do you want me to do, Artie?"

"What you do best, Catherine. My tournament starts at seven tonight. I want you to deal."

"Just deal?"

"Just deal."

"You have dealers."

"Not enough. And none of them have your special skills."

"Jesus, Artie, don't you ever do anything straight up?"

"I tried that, dear. It cost me a restaurant."

Cattie thought for a moment. "What's in it for me?"

31

(Denn)

OLD GAMBLERS ALWAYS HAVE A STORY OR
two about getting broke. Broke to where they can't
buy a cup of coffee. Broke to where they have to
leave town to avoid all the people they owe money
to. Old gamblers talk about getting broke the way
fishermen talk about the one that got away—each
one trying to top the other. Sammy Gold had told
Denn about being so broke he'd had to give blood
twice in one day to buy a thirty-dollar entry into a
holdem tournament. Cookie, an old poker player
Denn had known back in Fairview, had once raided
his grandson's piggy bank. Everybody had a story.

But not Denn. Not until now.

He had won his first hand of blackjack, picking
up two face cards, twenty points, then watching the
dealer bust out by drawing a ten to his thirteen.

"Let it ride," Denn had said, feeling like a character in a movie. That time he caught a seven, four.

He drew a queen and made twenty-one, beating the dealer's nineteen.

"Again," Denn said, betting all $6,400.

The dealer pitched him a nine, trey.

"Hit me," said Denn.

The dealer hit him. With a king.

Twenty-two points. Busted.

The funny thing was that Denn felt nothing. He turned away from the blackjack table and walked out of the casino to his car. He didn't feel a thing— no pain, no regret, no nothing. It was as if he didn't exist. He was invisible.

He got in his car and started it and looked at the gas gauge.

He didn't even have enough gas to make it to Hoover Dam.

32

(Cattie)

CATTIE WAS SOAKING IN THE BATHTUB WHEN she heard someone knocking at her door. She tried to think who it could be. The list was extremely short and included no one she cared to see. She closed her eyes, slid forward in the tub, and let the water cover everything but her mouth and nose. She stayed that way for several minutes, listening to the background hiss of the plumbing.

When she surfaced, whoever had been knocking had given up. She climbed out of the tub, dried herself, wrapped a towel around her head, and padded naked to her bedroom.

What was appropriate attire to help a scumbag like Artie Kingston win a poker tournament?

She sorted through her wardrobe, rejecting anything that had the slightest hint of personality. Something in beige, or taupe, or putty. She selected a pair of khaki slacks and a pale blue blouse, put them on, stood before the mirror on the bathroom door, and scowled at her reflection. All she needed was a minivan and a pair of brats and she could pass as a young soccer mom.

It didn't matter anyway. Artie would probably make her wear some doinky dealer uniform.

Whatever. For fifty grand she'd wear a pink tutu.

The clock beside her bed read 5:23. Time to go. Cattie slung her purse over her shoulder and grabbed her car keys from the kitchen counter. She opened the door, stepped out into the carpeted hallway, and froze.

Denn Doyle was sitting opposite her door, his back against the wall, long arms wrapped around his knees, right hand gripping his left wrist, looking up at her.

Cattie waited, expecting anything, expecting everything. But Denn didn't move or speak.

"Are you stalking me?" she asked.

Denn shrugged. "I don't know. Maybe. I have a question for you."

"What?"

"Did you really do it for the money?"

Cattie pictured the wad of hundreds propping up the table leg.

"Why? What does it matter?"

"Because if you did it for the money, then maybe I could understand."

Cattie took a breath. "I did it because that's what I do," she said.

Denn kept on staring at her.

"It's who I am," Cattie said.

Denn was shaking his head. "I don't believe you."

"It's true," Cattie said. "Just as well you found out when you did."

"Instead of when?"

"Instead of later."

"I still don't believe you," he said.

"That's your problem." Cattie closed her door and started toward the front entrance of the building. She heard him get to his feet, heard his footsteps following her. She stopped and whirled, facing him.

Denn stopped as if he'd hit an invisible wall.

"What do you want from me?" Cattie said.

Slowly, as if approaching a nervous rottweiler, Denn reached out a hand and lightly touched her cheek with his fingertips.

Cattie flinched but did not back away. His eyes were moving around her face in little jerks, as if he was memorizing every pore.

He flattened his palm and held it against her face. His hand felt cool at first but quickly warmed.

Cattie willed herself to slap it away, but her arm would not obey.

After several seconds Denn took his hand back.

"I don't care about the money," he said. "I just wanted to make sure you were okay."

"Of course I'm okay," she said, backing away from him, once again moving down the hallway. When was the last time anybody had cared that she was okay? "I can take care of myself," she said as she shoved open the lobby door.

As the door closed behind her, she heard him say, "I know you can."

33

(Denn)

DENN WAITED IN THE EMPTY HALLWAY,
giving Cattie time to get in her car and leave.

What had he learned? Maybe nothing. Maybe
she had told him the truth. She was just who she
was and there was nothing either of them could do
about it.

Cattie had once told him about her mother.
Growing up that way would mess up just about anybody. She had told him about her months working
the blackjack tables with Jerry Burkhardt. She had
told him about her shoplifting, and how a guy had
once offered her a thousand dollars to have sex with
him. She took the money—but ran before he could
touch her. She had told Denn all about herself, but
he had never thought that he would become one of
her victims.

Maybe she was right. Maybe it was just who she

was. Hooked on the action. Risk was her drug.

He thought about losing the last of his money at that blackjack table. He remembered how it had felt to make the decision to do something really stupid. To throw himself into the abyss. It had felt good. For a moment.

Maybe risk was *his* drug too.

After the blackjack disaster, Denn had gone for a long walk up the Strip, weaving his way through the throngs of tourists. He had walked for hours, knowing he should go home and sleep, but it was easier to let the rhythm of his steps pound the misery into his brain. When he got back to his car, late afternoon, all he could think to do was to see Cattie. To hurt himself more. To make himself feel.

He had always thought that kids who cut themselves were sick. Maybe he was a little sick too.

Now, standing in the hallway outside Cattie's apartment, sleepless and exhausted, he considered his options. Broke. No friends. Nothing but two weeks paid up on his apartment, and his Camaro. Obviously he would have to sell the car. He might be able to get ten thousand for it, enough to buy his way into the tournament. If he could find a buyer in the next hour. But even then, if he didn't win the tournament— which he had to admit was the most likely scenario— he would be reduced to begging on the street.

Denn took a deep breath as he felt himself come to a decision. He would go back to his apartment, get some much-needed sleep, and then sell his car in the morning. He would buy himself an old beater for a couple thousand, then invest the rest of the money in $15-$30 holdem games. Come back up through the ranks one hand at a time and not do anything stupid—like betting it all at the blackjack table.

Artie Kingston would have to wait.

Denn realized he was gritting his teeth hard enough to bust a molar. He opened his mouth and worked his jaw from side to side. Cattie would be gone by now, off to do whatever it was she did for Artie Kingston. Denn might never see her again.

I'm okay with that, he told himself. He walked down the hall and out the front entrance.

Cattie was sitting on the hood of his car, smoking a cigarette.

"I didn't know you smoked," Denn said. He was surprised at how normal his voice sounded.

"I just started. This guy was walking by and I asked him for a cigarette. He gave it to me." She puffed inexpertly on the cigarette. "I usually get what I ask for," Cattie said. "But I didn't ask for you."

Denn didn't know what she meant, so he waited.

"Are you playing in Artie's tournament tonight?" she asked.

Denn shook his head. "No money."

Cattie took another drag off the cigarette, scowled at it, and flicked it away.

"Would you play if you had some?" she asked.

Denn shrugged. "I don't know."

"Wait here," Cattie said. She ran back into the building.

34

(Jimbo)

I DON'T KNOW WHEN THE LAST BIG-MONEY freeze-out tournament was played in Vegas, but nobody I'm talking to can remember one. All the tournaments these days have a payout structure that rewards the top ten percent or so—in other words, if you've got a hundred players, the last ten standing all get a chunk of the prize pool. That's what we're used to.

But the Big Deal is winner take all, and that's got everybody pretty cranked because it's something new. Also, there's no house rake, so all the money collected goes to the winning player. In Vegas that's what you call a bargain.

We're milling around the fringes of the King's Crossing poker room, about a hundred twenty of us. The tournament is supposed to start in ten minutes; guys are starting to take their assigned seats. I'm looking around, checking out the other players. I see several former World Series of Poker champs: Chris Money-maker, Carlos Mortenson, Phil Hellmuth, and a few others. Annie Duke is there, and her brother, Howard Lederer. I see Sammy Gold and Lyle Berman and Del the Cabby and . . . I must know more than half of them. This is gonna be no walk in the park.

I'm thinking that maybe my 10K would have been better spent elsewhere.

Then I see Denn Doyle, and I'm sure of it.

The kid must have got himself a backer. And I turned him down. The situation reeks of bad karma. He'll probably be the one to bust me out of the tournament.

I walk over to him, shake his hand, and wish him luck. He has dark rings under his eyes and not much color in his face.

"Thanks, Jimbo. Good luck yourself."

I'm relieved that he doesn't seem to hold the nonloan against me. After all, it was just business.

"Glad to see you got your buy-in," I say.

The kid shrugs. "I got lucky."

"You look like hell."

"Haven't had a lot of sleep lately."

"You still interested in swapping action? Ten percent?"

He seems surprised. "Why would I do that?"

"So if I win you still get a piece of it, and vice versa. Why do you think?"

"Don't you plan to win?"

"Well, yeah, but . . ."

"I plan to win," he says. Then he grins and slaps me on the shoulder. "Anyway, good luck to you, Jimbo." And he walks away.

I'm kinda stung, but I know what he means. There's no winning a freeze-out tournament if you head into it with a second- or third-place mentality. It's balls-to-the-wall, take-no-prisoners, do-or-die poker.

35

(Denn)

THE SURGE OF BREEZY CONFIDENCE THAT had gotten him through the conversation with Jimbo Cowles left suddenly; Denn felt the thirty-odd hours he had gone without sleep from his eyeballs to his toes. And the tournament that was about to start would run for another twelve hours, maybe more. The plastic chit in his pocket—table 8, seat 6—felt like a slab of hot lead. He had paid $10,000 for it. In eight minutes he and nine other players would take their seats at table 8, hand their chits to the dealer, and look at their first hand. Ten other players at each of eleven other tables would be doing the same, all starting out equal, each with a theoretical one-in-120 chance to walk away with $1.2 million.

He had to be out of his mind. Some of the best players in the world were about to take their seats—and chances were they'd had plenty of sleep last night.

Denn walked out of the poker room and sat down at a bank of twenty-five-cent video-poker machines. He felt in his pocket for a quarter. Nothing. Just that $10,000 chit. He didn't play video poker anyway. Video poker was strictly for suckers. Speaking of which . . . there was an old Irish saying Denn had heard from his dad:

Fool me once, shame on you. Fool me twice, shame on me.

Was he being fooled again? Was Cattie setting him up? He couldn't imagine how. Or why. It was her money.

She had given him the 10K. Just handed it to him, like it was a handful of scrap paper.

"What do you want?" he had asked her, staring down at the thick sheaf of Franklins.

"Nothing," she had said.

"You want me to be your shill?"

"I told you, it's yours. Bet it on roulette if you want."

"I don't get it."

"You don't have to *get* anything. The money's yours. You should know one thing, though. I'll be one of the dealers in the tournament, and Artie expects me to give him some nice cards."

"Are you gonna do it?"

Cattie had shrugged. "You know me."

"Not really."

"I haven't decided."

"But you're bankrolling me to play in the tournament?"

"Then maybe I should deal *you* some winners."

"How about you just deal."

Cattie laughed. "You want my advice? Take the money and go back to Fairview. Of course, I know you won't."

With that she had walked quickly to her car and left him there.

Deeply suspicious, Denn had nevertheless driven straight to King's Crossing and entered himself in the Big Deal, at every moment expecting to be told the money was counterfeit, or be accused of stealing it, or have them refuse to accept his fake ID, or . . . He had no idea what game Cattie was playing.

Fool me twice . . .

Looking through the entrance to the poker room, he could see her in the dealer's seat at table 1, waiting, her lips faintly curved in a Mona Lisa smile. How could a girl so duplicitous look so innocent?

Why had she given him the money?

Denn again felt the chit in his pocket. Most of the players were sitting. Denn moved back into the poker room to find table 8, seat 6. The room was buzzing with dozens of conversations. Artie, wearing a gray suit to match his complexion, was standing at the podium holding a microphone. He tapped the mike sharply with his fingernail, and the conversations slackened.

"Good evening, all. Welcome to the King's Crossing's Big Deal freeze-out. I'm Art Kingston, and this is my operation."

He paused to let the last of the conversations die out, then continued.

"We are making history here tonight. The Big Deal is the first ever million-dollar-plus winner-take-all tournament. Second, third, or fourth place loses just as bad as if you're the first one knocked out. Wait, let me correct that—we do have a second-place prize." He held up a book. "Your very own copy of *Poker for Dummies.*"

A wave of subdued laughter rolled unevenly through the room.

"And, of course, our sympathies."

More weak laughter. Artie was no entertainer.

Denn found his seat. He only knew two of the other players at the table—Jen Harman and a small-time pro they called Comb-over Bob.

Artie was still talking. "Blinds will increase every hour at the breaks, and we keep playing till there's only one of you left—no matter how long it takes.

"I don't want to waste any more of your precious time, but I do want to point out that this is a no-rake, no-entry-fee promotional tournament. Every dollar goes to the winner. The house edge is that, win or lose, you will all go away knowing that King's Crossing has the best poker room in Vegas, hands down."

Scattered applause.

"Oh, and one more edge for the house. I'm playing too. And of course I plan to win."

Most of the players chuckled. They all had similar plans.

"The game is Texas holdem. If you have any questions, please direct them to Morty Deasel, our tournament director. Dealers? Shuffle up and deal. Let's get the cards in the air!"

36

(Denn)

THE EARLY STAGES OF A BIG-MONEY NO-LIMIT tournament are usually pretty boring. Nobody wants to get knocked out before they've had a chance to settle in and study the opposition. The Big Deal was no exception. In fact the players were even more cautious than usual.

Everybody started with $10,000 in tournament chips. The blind bets were at $10-$20, and would increase every hour. At Denn's table they played the first thirty hands without a showdown. Every pot was won on or before the flop. Denn managed to pick up a small pot when he flopped a king, six, trey to his ace, king. He bet half the pot, and the other players folded.

A few players—all from other tables—did not make it to the break. Denn watched one of them, a small-time pro named Bird Svenquist—stand up shakily and walk out of the room, his face bloodless and slack.

When the first break was announced, the coffee drinkers made a beeline for the rest rooms, the nicotine addicts lit up on their way to the smoking lounge, and the rest of the players wandered around the cardroom, checking out the stacks at the other tables and making small talk.

Artie Kingston was standing behind Cattie, chatting with Morty Deasel.

Denn still didn't know what Cattie was going to do. But he would find out: The dealers rotated from table to table every half hour. And as players started falling away, Morty Deasel would start consolidating tables. Sooner or later Cattie would be dealing him a hand.

"Dude, *¿cómo está?*"

"I'm hanging in there, Jimbo. You?"

"Just waiting for aces. Check out that pile, though." He pointed out a stack of chips at table 11 that looked like about $48,000. "College kid from UNLV," Jimbo said. "He doubled up twice, pocket jacks both times. First he catches a third jack to beat some poor sap with pocket queens. Second time he goes all-in under the gun, and Bird Svenquist calls him with pocket aces. The kid makes a straight on the river. Bye-bye, Birdie. The kid's been playing crazy ever since."

"He won't last," Denn said. Pocket jacks was not an all-in-quality hand this early in a tournament. The UNLV kid wouldn't stay lucky for long.

Jimbo smiled. "You got that right. I just hope I'm the one to show him the door."

As the blinds increased, more and more players were eliminated. Most of them were what the pros called "dead money"—players who never had a chance. But a few of the top players busted out as well. Todd Brunson, Miami John, Phil Ivey, and several other pros were gone before the third break. The field was soon down to seven tables, seventy players. Denn had built his stack up to a comfortable $60,000, thanks to the UNLV student, who first thing after moving to Denn's table had gone all-in for $34,000. Denn, with pocket aces, called him with his last $30,000. The kid turned up pocket tens. Denn's aces held up and he won the hand. The UNLV kid was still in the game, but he was down to his last $4000—the part of his stack Denn hadn't had enough chips to cover.

So far Denn had not noticed any funny business from the dealers. But Artie, still at table 6, had built his stack to well over $100,000, and was using his superior chip position to dominate the other players. He had built up his chip lead during the third round, when Cattie had been dealing at his table.

Denn looked around the room and spotted Cattie at table 5. Another round and she'd be taking her turn at his table.

"It's on you, sir," said the dealer.

Startled, Denn looked at the two cards he had been dealt. Jack, eight. He mucked them. He had let his mind wander. He'd have to watch that.

The UNLV kid raised all-in and was called by a stout, angry-looking man named Jacques or Jock or something like that. The kid turned up a six, eight and beat Jock's ace, king when two eights hit the board.

Denn smiled. He liked it when the weaker players won. He saw it as money in the bank.

Swept up in the rhythm of the cards, Denn forgot how long he had gone without sleep. He was playing as well as he ever had, picking up little pots at every opportunity, dodging the bullets that inevitably came his way, building his stack slowly and patiently, letting the other players make their mistakes.

He was so focused on the game, he almost didn't notice when Cattie sat down in the dealer's chair.

37

(Cattie)

AT FIRST ARTIE HAD SEEMED TO LIKE HIS
pocket aces. He had won a huge pot. He hadn't liked
it as much when Cattie dealt him the same two
black aces the very next hand. But he had won
another nice pot. When she gave him the same two
cards the third time running, Artie mucked them
before the flop and gave her a look that would have
scared her if she gave a damn what happened to her.

But she didn't. She smiled, then dealt him the
same two black aces a fourth time. Artie mucked
them, then folded the next several hands, until
Cattie was rotated to the next table.

At the break Morty took her aside.

"Very funny," he said.

"What?" Giving him her innocent look.

"You know damn well what. You think anybody's gonna believe it, he keeps showing them

same two black aces? Get your head in the game, sweetie. You do not want to get on Mr. Kingston's bad side."

"He has a good side?"

Morty snorted and sent her back to her table.

Another couple hours and she would be dealing at Artie's table again. She wondered what she was going to do.

38

(Jimbo)

YOU LIKE BAD-BEAT STORIES?

Me neither. But listen to this. I'm looking at the king, queen of spades and raise preflop for $1000, trying to buy the blinds. I get one caller, the UNLV kid. *Okay,* I think, *things could still work out for me here.*

The flop comes jack of spades, ten of spades, deuce of hearts. I shove in my last $5500, thinking the UNLV kid will probably fold.

Wouldn't you know it, the kid calls me.

Since I'm all-in and there can be no more betting, we turn up our cards. He's got a pair of red eights.

With two cards to come, I'm better than fifty-fifty. Any spade will give me a flush. Any ace or nine will give me the nut straight. And a king or a queen will give me the winning pair. That's twenty-two outs, and two cards to hit one of them.

The dealer flips up the turn card: seven of hearts. The dealer hesitates for a few seconds, giving us a little drama that I do not appreciate, then deals the river.

Four of clubs. It takes me about three seconds to realize I'm beat.

"Nice hand," I say. I get up from the table and walk away.

Here's the thing: There is nothing quite like the feeling of betting.

And there is nothing like the feeling of betting and winning.

And there is nothing like the feeling of betting and losing.

Those are the three basic buzzes make it worth getting out of bed most days. Each one's different, and none of them is any good without the other two. They are like hot dog, bun, and mustard. Winning would be no fun if you never lost. Betting would be no fun without the risk. And losing—nongamblers don't get this—losing is not so bad. It actually can feel good, in a way, the way it feels good to peel off a scab or confess a sin.

When a gambler loses, he feels he has paid a price. He thinks it improves his odds on the next wager. Even though we all know it's a bunch of crap, we believe deep down that losing is the price of winning.

So how come I don't feel better?

I stand behind the rail and look out over the remaining players. Five minutes ago I was in the middle of it. Now it looks unreal, a fantasy world.

I see Denn's shock of black hair sticking up a little higher than the rest. Maybe he'll win the thing.

Maybe I should have bankrolled him.

Too late now.

39

(Denn)

THERE ARE TIDES IN A POKER TOURNAMENT.
Sometimes, when hopes are high and the chips are
flowing, hardly a minute goes by without a dealer
calling out, "Player down," sending another slump-
shouldered player to the rail. Then there are other
times when nobody gets knocked out for half an
hour or more, as the players hunch protectively over
their stacks, taking no chances, waiting for somebody else to do something stupid.

Sensing these ebbs and flows was one of the keys
to winning. When the players were defensive and
fearful, Denn knew to start stealing small pots: raise
with something like jack, nine and watch them fold,
fold, fold. But when the tide turned and a wave of
suicidal optimism swept through the room, he
would lie back and let them cut each other to bits.

Cattie took the dealer's seat during one of the
fast times, when everybody seemed to be on tilt.

Denn picked up a few weak hands that he was happy to fold. Layne Flack went all-in with pocket kings and got knocked out by the UNLV kid, who caught an ace on the flop to go with his ace, jack suited. Denn was not sorry to see Layne go—he was one of the strongest tournament players in the world.

A few hands later Denn found himself with a pair of red aces in the hole. Pocket aces, on average, showed up only once every two hundred twenty hands. He stared at his cards for a long time, wondering whether Cattie knew what she had dealt him.

"It's on you," Cattie said.

Denn raised to $1800, three times the big blind.

Everybody folded.

The next hand he picked up pocket kings. He looked at Cattie, caught her eye, and mucked his cards.

Cattie raised her left eyebrow about a millimeter.

Denn got up and walked away from the table. He had a big enough stack that he could afford to miss a few hands. He went to the rest room and washed his hands and face, then examined himself in the mirror.

He looked like hell—pasty skin, circles under his eyes, and three days of scanty beard growth. Funny thing was, he felt fine while he was sitting at the table, but now, looking at himself, he felt like the walking dead.

By the time he got back, the blinds had increased to $500-$1000, another player had bitten the dust, and his table was breaking up. Morty was handing out table chits and directing the remaining players to empty seats at the other tables. They were down to three tables now. Artie was the chip leader with more than $270,000, close to a quarter of all the chips in play. The UNLV kid had enjoyed another run of luck and was sitting on about $190,000. Denn, with $118,000, was a distant third. About five of the remaining players were down to the felt, with too few chips to make it through a round of blinds.

It was desperation time—there would be a lot of crazy play this round.

Denn racked his chips, moved to his new table, and sat down with Jen Harman on his right and the UNLV kid on his left.

The dealer was a rangy, mustached man with thinning gray hair whose name badge read TEX. Tex dealt the cards with the precision and speed of one who has done nothing but deal for half a century. Denn let his first several hands go, then found himself with an ace, king under the gun. He raised Jen Harman's blind to $4000. The UNLV kid called, and everybody else, including Jen, folded.

The flop came jack, nine, trey in three different suits. Denn checked. The UNLV kid bet $20,000.

Denn's first impulse was to fold, but he gave himself a moment to think. Twenty grand was a big bet. Too big. Clearly, the UNLV kid did not want a call. That could mean he had nothing. Or maybe he had something weak like a small pair, or a nine, or even a trey. Any of which would beat Denn's ace high.

It was also possible that the UNLV kid had a legitimate hand and had overbet the pot to make Denn think he was trying to buy it. But that didn't seem likely. From what Denn had seen, the kid was not that sophisticated. The $20,000 was probably an attempt at a buy. If Denn folded, the kid would be raising him at every opportunity.

Denn counted out $50,000, half his stack, and pushed it out.

The UNLV kid thought for a long time, then shrugged and folded, throwing his cards away face-up. A pair of sixes.

Denn felt his heart begin to race. That was what happened when he gambled and won. Dead calm while the hand was in play, but as soon as it was over his heart would start pounding.

It felt good.

40

(Cattie)

BY THE TIME SHE GOT ROTATED BACK TO Artie's table, he was looking more corpselike than ever. That probably meant he was feeling pretty good. He gave her a look—a tight smile with the eyebrows slightly elevated—that she interpreted to mean *Do Not Disappoint Me*.

Cattie shuffled the cards and dealt. Artie had so many chips, he had a good shot at winning the tournament without her help.

On the third hand two aces hit the board on the flop. It was a nothing hand—Sammy Gold bet out on the flop and everybody folded—but when Cattie scooped up the cards, she put the aces on the bottom of the deck and performed a false cut to keep them there. Knowing where the aces were was the key to controlling the action.

What she would do with that knowledge was another matter entirely.

Cattie continued to deal, picking up another ace on the next hand and the fourth ace a few hands later. She kept all four aces out of play for the next several hands, until one of the players said, "Aren't there any aces in this deck?"

The next hand she flopped three aces.

"There they are," said Sammy Gold, laughing. Sammy had been playing poker since the 1960s. Nothing surprised him anymore.

Artie was giving her that look again.

Cattie dealt the fourth ace on the turn, and even Sammy's eyebrows shot up. He won the pot with his king kicker.

Cattie mixed the aces back into the deck and dealt a random hand. She felt a tap on her shoulder. It was Sandee Roode, one of the other dealers.

"Morty says you need a break."

"I don't, actually," said Cattie, avoiding Artie's eyes.

"Morty says."

Cattie squared up the deck and gave up her seat.

Morty was watching. He crooked a finger, summoning her to the dais.

"You are some piece of work," he said.

"That's what I hear."

"I got some advice for you, sweetie. Take that ten grand I gave you and use it to buy yourself a ticket to Alaska."

"Why Alaska?"

"On account of Artie don't like the cold."

"Maybe I'll just go back to Minnesota."

"That might work," Morty said. "As long as you go."

"I think I'll stick around and see who wins this thing."

Morty shrugged. "It's no skin off my ass."

41

(Denn)

TWO THIRTY A.M., DOWN TO TWO TABLES, six players at one and five at the other, blinds at $2000-$4000. Artie, still the chip leader, was sitting on half a million in chips. Denn, at the other table, had $260,000. He had hit his second or third wind around midnight. As long as he stayed focused on the game, his lack of sleep didn't bother him, but when he looked up from the table, the cardroom took on an eerie, dreamlike, underwater look.

Stay in the game. That was all he had to do— outlast them all.

Half an hour later the UNLV kid went all-in for $22,000 with a pair of fives. Artie called with ace, ten and caught a ten on the turn, sending the kid to the rail. With only ten players left, Morty had them all draw cards to select their seats for the final table, and they took a ten-minute break.

"Blinds are $4000-$8000," Morty announced. "From here on we play straight through—no more breaks till we're down to the final two players."

"What if I got to piss?" complained Sammy Gold.

"You miss a hand or two."

"Don't worry, Sammy, you won't last that long," said Freddie Simm, a low-limit bottom-feeder who had lucked his way to the final table.

Artie, looking half dead as always, went over to the lounge area and lit a cigarette. Denn looked around the room and spotted Cattie sitting at one of the empty tables. He took the seat next to her.

"I noticed Morty pulled you out of the rotation," he said.

"I guess he didn't like it when I gave Artie pocket aces five hands in a row."

Denn laughed. "He's built up a pretty good lead."

Cattie nodded. "Yeah, but he's on his own now."

"You sure?"

"No."

They sat together without speaking until the break ended. Every now and then Artie would look at them from the lounge.

Their new dealer, a young Cambodian woman named Ree, cut the deck and dealt. Artie was sitting in the two seat—two seats to the dealer's left. Denn was in the five seat, directly across from the dealer. It was the first time Denn and Artie had been at the same table. All the big-name players had been knocked out. It was down to Denn, Artie, Sammy Gold, Freddie Simm, and six players Denn didn't know.

Denn watched Ree carefully, trying to figure out if she was working the deck to Artie's advantage.

A few hands later Artie lost a big hand to Sammy Gold, making Denn think that maybe Ree was dealing a straight game. Maybe Cattie was the only mechanic in Artie's roster.

Freddie Simm raised all-in with a pair of tens and was knocked out by a young Hispanic kid named Angel. Down to nine.

On the very next hand the guy in the number-seven seat, a graybeard who claimed to be a gold miner from Alaska, shoved in his whole stack, $19,000. To his left a young Asian woman who called herself Kimkim made a sputtering sound with her lips and threw in her last $600. Denn called them and flipped up an ace, queen of hearts. The gold miner scowled and turned up an ace, jack. Kimkim showed a pair of deuces.

The flop came queen, jack, seven. Denn's pair of queens held up, and they were down to seven.

• • •

On the hour, Tex replaced Ree as the dealer. The blinds increased to $8000-$16,000. Once again Denn watched carefully, looking for signs that Tex was manipulating the deck. Artie had been playing very few hands. If Tex was a mechanic, he was too good for Denn to spot.

It took less than an hour to eliminate the next four players. Artie, with half the chips at the table, had been playing very few hands. Sammy Gold was sitting on $320,000. He had made a nice comeback. Denn, riding out a long dry spell, was down to $210,000. The fourth remaining player, an intense-looking lawyer from Seattle, had the remaining $70,000.

With the lawyer in the big blind, Artie made a big raise—$60,000—from under the gun. Sammy and Denn folded. The lawyer thought about it for almost two minutes. Calling the bet would put him all-in.

"You might as well call me," Artie said to him. "Blinds are going up again in five minutes. Time to make your move."

"I know," said the lawyer. "But I only got a jack, eight offsuit."

"I have a pair of sixes. You catch either one of your cards, you win. You're almost fifty-fifty."

The lawyer shrugged, turned up his jack, eight, and shoved in the last of his chips.

Tex dealt out the flop: jack, eight, ace.

"See?" said Artie. "Good call. I only have two outs. I need a six to beat you."

The turn card was a six, giving Artie trips.

"Ouch," said Artie. "That must hurt."

The lawyer slunk off, and they were down to three.

Sammy Gold had been playing great all night, dodging and weaving and making the most of it when he caught a hand or sensed weakness. Denn was impressed. Sammy had always struck him as an overly conservative player, but Sammy, realizing that in this tournament second place was just as bad as one-hundredth place, had loosened up his game.

With only three of them left, nearly every hand was decided before the flop. It was raise, fold, fold. Or raise, reraise, fold, fold. Or raise, reraise, raise all-in, fold, fold.

Denn was doing his own dodging and weaving, hoping for a confrontation between Artie and Sammy, which would either knock Sammy out or take Artie out of the lead.

The hand came up abruptly, as they always do. Sammy, under the gun, raised two times the big blind: $50,000.

That was a mistake, Denn thought. *He should have gone all-in.*

Unless he had a big hand and was trying to lure one of them into the pot thinking they could buy a cheap flop.

Denn looked at his own cards. Pocket queens.

Damn. With only three players, pocket queens was a powerhouse.

Artie called Sammy's bet. It was an odd call. Denn would have expected either a raise or a fold from Artie.

He thought back over the hand. Sammy had bet without hesitation, and his nostrils had flared slightly as he did so. A few weeks ago that would have meant that Sammy had a big hand—probably aces or kings. But Sammy had since been clued in that Denn could read those tells. Still, Sammy was tired—they were all tired. Maybe his actions had been unconscious. Or maybe he had found out that Denn knew that he knew that Denn could read his tells, and he really did have a big hand.

And what did Artie's call mean? Another big hand?

Denn looked at Ree, who had replaced Tex as dealer. Could this be the big setup? Give all three of them big pocket pairs, then arrange for Artie to hit his set?

Denn took one last look at his queens and pitched them into the muck.

The flop came queen, jack, six.

Oh, well.

Sammy, without hesitation, shoved out all his chips.

Artie said, "I call." He flipped up pocket jacks, giving him a set of jacks.

Sammy closed his eyes, drew a ragged breath, and turned up pocket aces.

The turn and river cards did not help him, and Sammy was history.

"Ten-minute break," Morty announced.

"You can go pee now, Sammy," Artie said.

42

(Denn)

DENN PUSHED HIS CHAIR BACK AND STOOD
up. He was surprised to find that the room was
almost empty. For a while the players who had been
knocked out had hung around, either playing in
side games or watching the tournament from the
rail. But now most of them had gone home. Only a
couple dozen tired looking railbirds were there, and
four dealers were waiting for their rotation to come
up. He spotted Jimbo Cowles's bowler hat at the
back of the room. Jimbo was talking to Sammy Gold,
no doubt swapping bad-beat stories.

Cattie was gone.

Denn walked through the sparsely populated slot
area to the front door and out into the parking lot. The
sky was getting bright behind Frenchman Mountain to
the east. How odd that morning should ever come to
Las Vegas, the city without clocks. Denn stretched and
blinked and tasted the air—once-clean desert air that

rolled into the city only to be soiled with auto exhaust and the underlying scent of despair.

What am I doing here? he wondered. *Is this real?*

He looked back at Artie Kingston's converted Kmart. He sniffed his armpit and ran his tongue around his mouth. Yuck. How long had it been since he had eaten? How many hours had he gone without sleep? Forty? Fifty? He wasn't sure. What time does the sun rise in Vegas? He had no idea. He had never seen a sunrise in Vegas. He wouldn't see one today, either.

Back inside, Artie was sitting at the table. Still no Cattie.

"Just in time, kid," he said. "Let's get this done."

"Blinds are still twenty-five and fifty thousand," Morty announced. "Get 'em in the air."

Heads-up poker is a game of pure aggression and dumb luck. Artie, with nearly a million, had Denn, with only $200,000, seriously out-chipped. Denn would need some amazing cards to overcome Artie's lead. Or Artie would have to catch some really bad ones. Or Artie would have to do something incredibly stupid.

Ree was dealing. Denn had pretty much decided that she was not fixing the deck. If she had been, he would have been eliminated long before. Artie must have been counting on Cattie to give him his edge. And maybe she had, early on. But now he was on his own.

The first hand, Denn picked up a pair of sixes and shoved in all his chips.

Artie thought about it for a few seconds. "What do you have, kid?"

"Don't know. Didn't look at my cards."

"Yeah, right." Artie mucked.

Denn's stack was now $250,000.

The next hand, Artie put in a big raise. Denn would have to go all-in to call. He looked at his cards. Jack, three. He folded.

On the next hand Denn raised all-in again, this time with a jack, queen of hearts.

Artie folded.

For the next several hands, they went back and forth, taking turns buying the blinds. Denn was amazed that Artie never called his raises. With such a large stack, Artie wouldn't need much of a hand to make a call on the correct play.

He sat back and studied his opponent.

What he saw surprised him.

He had been thinking of Artie Kingston as a stone cold reptile in human form. A force of nature. But what he saw now was a very tired man, not very healthy, who was afraid to lose.

Denn looked at his next hand. King, ten offsuit. How good a hand would Artie have to have to call him if he raised? Denn had a bad feeling. Something in Artie's body language set off warning bells in Denn's head. He folded. Artie gave off a bitter laugh and showed pocket kings.

Denn gave himself a mental pat on the back for making a perfect read.

Three hands later Artie looked carefully at Denn's stacks of chips, counted out exactly $194,000 from his own stacks, and pushed them out.

Was he buying the blinds again?

And why had he counted off the exact amount of chips he needed to put Denn all-in? Usually at this stage of a tournament a player would just say "All-in," and his declaration would be binding. The fact that Artie had counted out his chips so carefully meant something—but what?

The most likely answer was that Artie was showing off, rubbing it in that he could put Denn all-in without making much of a dent in his own stack. Or it could mean he was feigning confidence with a weak hand. Or that he was pretending to feign confidence, and that he actually had a powerhouse. Or that he was pretending to pretend to pretend . . .

Denn looked at his hand. Ace, jack.

If he folded now, he'd be down to less than $200,000. With the blinds at $25,000-$50,000, that wouldn't last long. He had to make a move, and he might not see another hand as good as ace, jack.

Besides, his gut told him that Artie was bluffing.

"I call," Denn said, laying his cards faceup on the table.

Artie shrugged and turned up a three, two. "Good call, kid," he said.

The dealer flopped a queen, queen, two, giving Artie a pair of deuces.

"Oops," Artie said.

Denn needed an ace or a jack to win. Six cards out of forty-four.

Denn felt the hope draining out of him. He started to stand up, ready to collect his copy of *Poker for Dummies* and walk away, when Ree dealt the turn card. An ace. A big, beautiful, black ace.

Denn sat back down. The advantage was his. Artie needed a third deuce to win.

Ree dealt out the river card. Denn stared at it, not quite understanding what he was seeing. He heard Artie cough, and a mutter of voices from the rail.

Was that really a third deuce?

It was. He felt his spine crumbling.

"Good game, kid," Artie said.

Denn, paralyzed, was unable to reply, as Ree went through the formality of counting out the chips Artie had bet, then counting out Denn's chips. Denn stared at her hands, at the chips, at the green felt tabletop. His brain had turned to fuzz, and he didn't understand what Ree was saying when she shoved the chips to Artie.

All but one gray $1000 chip.

"Your blind, sir," she said to Denn.

Denn said, "What?"

Ree was already shuffling the deck, getting ready to deal another hand. He could hear laughter coming from the rail. He looked at Artie, whose gray face actually had some color in it for a change.

"Where did that chip come from?" Artie said. "I put him all-in."

Ree paused, squaring up the deck. "I'm sorry, Mr. Kingston. You did not bet enough chips to put him all-in." She pointed at the lone gray chip in front of Denn. "He still has one thousand-dollar chip."

"He was hiding that chip. That's against tournament rules," Artie said.

Ree looked at Morty, who had been watching the action along with several others. As tournament manager, it was Morty's call.

Morty cleared his throat. "Uh, it was there, Mr.

Kingston. I guess you just didn't see it. Or you mis-
counted when you made your bet. You should have
just shoved your whole stack in."

Artie's face went hard; then he shrugged. "I
guess I have to beat you all over again, kid."

Denn picked up the gray chip. One thousand
dollars against $1,199,000. What were his chances
now? "You must now go all-in on the small blind,
sir," Ree said to Denn.

With only a thousand, and the blinds at twenty-
five and fifty thousand, he would have to go all-in
on every hand. He would have to win seven times in
a row just to build his stack high enough to cover
the blinds.

Denn looked over his shoulder at the guys lining
the rail.

Jimbo gave him a thumbs-up and said, "You got
him on the run now, kid."

Everybody laughed, even Artie.

Denn looked around the room at the sea of
empty tables and saw Cattie sitting at one of them,
arms crossed, looking straight at him, smiling.
When had she returned? And what was that around
her neck?

"Blinds, please," said the dealer.

Denn felt it again, the silent click of something
opening deep in his chest, and once again he felt

himself falling forward into the abyss. Maybe he had been falling his entire life.

It would take a miracle to win, but miracles happened every day in Vegas.

He had once watched a man win nine hands of blackjack in a row.

Artie sat back in his chair and lit a cigarette, in violation of his own rules.

Denn looked over at Cattie. She smiled, then reached up to touch the gold necklace.

"Your small blind, sir," said Ree.

Denn flipped his last chip into the air, caught it, and tossed it onto the felt.

"All-in," he said.

Epilogue

(Jimbo)

I'M PICKING UP A FEW POTS IN A SLEEPY little $5-$10 no-limit game at the Sand Dunes, up about fifteen hundred bucks, when I notice this red-head walk by, and that reminds me of Cattie Hart, and that makes me think of Denn Doyle, who I haven't thought about in months, and I say to this grumpy old guy sitting next to me, "Want to hear a story?"

"What kind of story you got that I want to hear, kid?" he asks.

"A story about a hand that happened right here at this very table, sir," I say, ever the Polite Young Man.

"This a bad-beat story? I've heard more bad-beat stories than you got hairs on your head, kid."

"You never heard one like this."

"They're all the same, kid. You get to be my age, you'll see it. Every time the same. Over and over.

Fifty-two cards in the deck and ten morons sitting around a table shoving money back and forth. You want to hear a bad-beat story? I played; I lost. The end. How do you like it?"

"Okay, okay," I say. "Whatever."

So I leave the grumpy old dude to his grumpy old thoughts and play a couple of hands I maybe shouldn't, and all of a sudden I'm down to my original 5K, and I figure it's time to go home before I find myself with a brand-new bad-beat story nobody wants to hear.

But before I can stand up, the dealer sends me two black queens.

I don't know about you, but when I get dealt pocket queens in no-limit holdem I feel this cold, clammy sensation on the back of my neck, like I'm getting breathed on by a corpse, and I figure I'm going to get drawn out on by some idiot playing ace, rag. Of course, queens is still a pretty good hand, and it needs defending, so when old grumpy bets out, I kick it up a couple hun.

He kicks me back $1000.

The clammy feeling is worse than ever now, but I still think I have the best hand. Grumpy's bet is too big. He doesn't want me to call, which probably means he has something like ace, king, or a middle pair. I figure I'd better shut him down right away before he has a chance to draw out on me, so I put my hands behind my stack and shove it in, the whole five.

When I see the shock and awe on his grumpy features I feel much better. No way can he call that bet. He knows it, and he knows I know it. He stares at me. I wait for him to fold.

And then he don't.

"Call," he says, and turns up the ace, king of hearts.

I show my queens. Now it's a coin toss, more or less. To beat me all he needs is any ace, or any king. I think he's about a two percent dog.

I tug my bowler hat low over my eyes and wait for the flop.

Every gambler's got a story. A story that sums up who they really are, and how they been running. Some stories are better than others. Denn Doyle has a pretty good one. I wonder if he's telling it now, wherever he is.

My story? Grumpy caught his king on the flop. The rest of it? You don't want to know, Bro.

Glossary

All-in. To bet all the money you have on the table. "He went *all-in* with a pair of deuces!"

Bad beat. When a strong hand loses to a longshot draw.

Blind. A forced bet that a player must post before the cards are dealt. In most holdem games there are two blind bets: the "small blind" and the "big blind." The big blind is usually double the small blind.

Boat. A full house. Also called a "full boat."

Button (or dealer button). A white plastic disc used to indicate which player acts last. After each hand the dealer moves the button to the next player.

Call. To match a bet.

Case card. The last card of a rank. "I had trip sevens, he had trip deuces, and he caught the *case deuce* on the river!"

Check. To decline to bet.

Fade. To cover another player's bet. A term usually used in the game of craps.

Flop. The first three upcards (community cards used by all active players) in a hand of holdem. Can be used as a verb: "I *flopped* a set of tens!"

Fold. To drop out of a hand.

Gut shot. A draw to an inside straight.

Heads-up. A poker hand involving only two players.

Heater. A run of winning hands. Also called a "rush."

Holdem. The most popular poker game in the world. Also called Texas Holdem.

Hole (or hole cards). A player's downcards.

Muck. 1) The pile of dead cards that players have folded during a hand. 2) To fold a hand.

Offsuit. Two cards of different suits. "He had an ace, king *offsuit*."

Omaha. A form of holdem in which each player receives four hole cards, and must use exactly two of them to make up a five-card hand. Omaha is most often played high-low split.

Pocket pair. In holdem, when you have two hole cards of the same rank, you have a pocket pair. "I was dealt *pocket aces*."

Quads. Four of a kind.

Rag. A low card that does not seem to help any of the players.

Raise. To bet more chips than the previous bettor, as in, "She bet five dollars, so I raised her another five."

River. The fifth and last upcard in holdem. Can be

used as a verb, especially when the last card is bad news, as in, "I got *rivered*!"

Sandbag. To check, then raise when your opponent bets. Also called a "check-raise."

Set. Three of a kind. Usually used when a player has a pocket pair and catches a third card of that rank. "I flopped a *set* of nines."

Suited. Two cards of the same suit. "He had an ace, king *suited*."

Tell. A mannerism or action by which a player unintentionally reveals something about his hand.

Tilt. When a player begins to gamble wildly, calling and raising foolishly, he is said to be *on tilt*. Also called "steaming."

Turn. The fourth upcard in holdem. Can be used as a verb, as when the turn card gives a player a good hand: "I *turned* a pair of kings."

Whipsaw. When a player with a moderately good hand is caught between two aggressive players who are raising back and forth, one of whom is likely to have a *very* good hand.

Wired. A pocket pair: "I bet my *wired aces* and everybody folded."

The Ranking of Poker Hands

All poker hands in holdem are composed of five cards. Higher ranked cards beat lower ranked cards.

Straight flush. Five sequential cards of the same suit. The best possible hand is an ace-high straight flush, also known as a "royal" flush. (A♥-K♥-Q♥-J♥-10♥)

Four-of-a-kind. Four cards of the same rank, with any other card. (K-K-K-K-x)

Full house. Three-of-a-kind and a pair in the same hand. (A-A-A-J-J)

Flush. Five cards of the same suit. (A♥-7♥-2♥-9♥-J♥)

Straight. Five cards in sequence. Aces can be used for high or low. (Both A-2-3-4-5 and 10-J-Q-K-A are considered straights.)

Three-of-a-kind. Three cards of the same rank, with any two other cards. (J-J-J-x-y)

Two pair. Two pairs of cards, with any other unmatched card. (K-K-J-J-x or 10-10-5-5-x)

Pair. Any two identically ranked cards, with any other three cards. (A-A-x-y-z, 4-4-x-y-z, etc.)

High card. If none of the above hands applies, the hand with highest card wins.

Here's a sneak peek of
Pete Hautman's next book

BLANK CONFESSION

Available now

Shayne Blank walks into the police station and confesses to having killed someone.

How could the quiet, unassuming new kid in town be a murderer? It's hard to believe, but as Shayne tells his story, Detective Rawls is forced to face the reality that Shayne may be more—a lot more—than he seems.

But who is he?

Five lousy minutes.

Detective George Rawls hung up the phone, brought his feet down from his cluttered desktop, looked at his watch, and sighed. If the kid had walked into the station five minutes later, Rawls's shift would have been over. He would have been driving home to enjoy a peaceful dinner with his wife.

Five more minutes and Benson would have caught this case. Rawls stood up and looked over the divider toward Rick Benson's desk. Benson, looking back at him, smirked. Rawls rolled his eyes and hitched up his pants. They kept falling down—his wife's fault, all those vegetables she'd been feeding him since his cholesterol numbers came in high.

He opened the upper left-hand drawer of his desk and took out his service revolver. Rawls was old school; he still used the weapon that had been issued to him as a rookie. He emptied the cylinder into the drawer and slid the unloaded weapon into his shoulder holster.

The unloaded gun was a prop. These young punks were impressed by such things. Most of them. He left his jacket hanging on the back of his chair and made his way out of the room and down the hallway toward the front entrance. He walked past the long citizens' bench, automatically checking out the four people sitting there: A slight, pale-faced boy—black jeans, black T-shirt, scuffed-up black cowboy boots—sat with his elbows resting on his knees, staring at the floor. Probably some middle-school bad boy picked up for shoplifting. Next was a young woman wearing a tight skirt, smeared mascara, and a nasty bruise on her right cheek. A hooker, no doubt. Then an anxious-looking older woman, probably there to report a runaway husband, or a purse snatching. At the end was a scowling middle-aged man in a rumpled suit—could be anything.

Rawls made these assessments automatically and effortlessly. Part of the job.

Directly facing the front doors of the police station, John Kramoski sat behind his elevated desk flipping through the duty roster. Rawls stopped in front of him. The desk sergeant looked up.

"Sorry, George," Kramoski said. "I know your shift is almost over, but you were up. And it's a kid—your specialty."

Rawls was the precinct's unofficial "Youth Crimes" officer. He had once believed that, working with kids, he might actually make a difference. These days he wasn't so sure.

"Where is he?" he asked.

Kramoski jerked his thumb toward the bench.

Rawls looked over, surprised. "How come he's not in the interview room?"

"He walked in here by himself. Besides, look at him. What's he gonna do?"

"We're talking about the kid on the end, right?"

"Yep."

Rawls shook his head. "He looks, like, twelve."

"Says he's sixteen."

"Jesus."

"And Mary and Joseph, bro." Kramoski returned his attention to the duty roster.

Rawls walked back down the hall, past the man in the suit, past the older woman, past the prostitute. He stopped in front of the kid and waited for him to look up. It took a few seconds. The kid's hair was thick, the color of dried leaves, maybe three weeks past needing a cut. He slowly sat back and raised his head to look directly into Rawls's eyes, his expression devoid of all emotion.

Rawls felt something throb deep within his gut. He had seen that expression before, on other faces. The face of a mother who had lost her only child. The face of a man who had just learned he would be spending the rest of his life in prison. The face of a girl who woke up to find that she would never walk again. A look of despair so deep and profound . . . it was as if the connections between the mind and the face were severed, leaving only a terrible blankness.

He had seen that expression in other places too. The morgue. Funeral parlors. Murder scenes.

The face of the dead.

But this boy was not dead. Somewhere behind those eyes there existed a spark—a spark that had brought him here, to this building, to this bench, to George Rawls.

"Are you Shayne?" Rawls asked.

The boy dropped his chin. Rawls took that as a yes and sat beside him on the bench, feeling every last one of his forty-three years, fifteen of them as a cop. Despite having conducted hundreds of such interviews, he found himself at a loss. Something about this kid—who could not have weighed much more than his Labrador retriever—frightened him. Not fear for himself. The other kind of fear: fear that the universe no longer made sense, that everything was about to change.

"So . . . ," Rawls cleared his throat, looking straight ahead, ". . . who did you kill?"

I met Shayne the same day I got busted for having drugs in my locker, which was also the day after this huge thunderstorm that knocked over a bunch of trees, including the giant elm in our backyard.

I was walking to school. I had left home early so I could look at the storm damage. I could hear chain saws from every direction. Each block had three or four trees down. Some had fallen on houses, some against power lines, and there was even one big oak tree completely blocking Thirty-first Street.

None of the buses had arrived yet when I got to the school. As I started up the wide, shallow steps leading to the front door I heard a humming, burbling sound and looked back to see a motorcycle pull up to the curb. A battered BMW, at least thirty years old. The tank and fenders were painted primer gray. The seat was patched with duct tape. The rider, dressed in a black T-shirt and black jeans, put down the kickstand and took off his helmet.

My first thought: *He looks too young to have a driver's license.*

He ran his fingers through his hair, hung his helmet

on the mirror, looked at me, looked at the school, looked back at me.

"Nice suit," he said. He had a soft, crisp voice, and some kind of accent.

"Thanks." I was wearing my dark gray three-button, the one with the cuffed trousers. "Nice bike," I said. I can be a little sarcastic sometimes.

He looked down at his battered motorcycle. "Not really." He gestured at the school building. "You go here?"

"Why else would I be here?"

He nodded. "Me too. I just moved here. I start today. Where's the student parking?" Definitely an accent—maybe southern, but with a sharp edge to it.

"See that sign?" I pointed. "That huge sign that says STUDENT PARKING?"

"Oh," he said.

Once again looking at my suit, he said, "Is there, like, a dress code or something?"

I took in his frayed T-shirt, his holey jeans, his beat-up black cowboy boots. "Lucky for you, no. As long as you don't wear gang colors or a T-shirt with swear words."

He nodded. "So what's with the suit?" He didn't ask it meanly, just in a mildly curious way.

"Some people like to dress nice," I said.

He nodded as if he understood, popped the helmet back on his head, turned the bike around, and rode off toward the parking lot.

I didn't even know his name, but already I liked him.

Mi nombre es Miguel Martín, and no, I am not Mexican. Actually, I am Haitian on my mom's side. Her parents came from Haiti back in 1971. They speak Haitian French. I am learning Spanish, however. My mom wanted me to learn French, but learning Spanish is more useful on account of I am often mistaken for Mexican, even by Mexicans, which is weird because Pépé—Mom's dad—is black. That deep purple-black skin color that comes from the west coast of Africa via Haiti. My grandmother, Mémé, is freckled, red-headed, and white. Her ancestors sailed to Haiti from France back in the 1600s. That's her story, anyway. These days her red hair is from a dye bottle, but she claims it's her real color.

My mom turned out to be a medium-brown-skinned woman with Afro hair that turns reddish in the summer. My dad is white, third or fourth generation Italian American.

Anyway, when all those genes got mixed up, I somehow came out looking Mexican. Imagine a Mexican kid, kind of small, wearing a suit and oversize tortoiseshell glasses. That's me. My sister, Marie—we're in the same grade even though she's ten months older than me—has light skin and our grandma's freckles, but her features are more African-looking.

My real name is Mike Martin, aka Mikey the Munchkin, and a *bueno día* is any day I don't feel the need to slink, or, in *español, escabullirse.* Do you know about slinking? It's a way of moving from place to place so people don't notice you. Cats are very good at it. Rats are even better. Lions and polar bears never slink. Okay, maybe a little, but only when they're sneaking up on you.

I have noticed that most short guys (I am the shortest guy in the eleventh grade) adopt one of two strategies. Some, like Chris Rock, or Prince, or Napoleon, have these enormous, noisy egos and make up for their lack of size by dressing and talking big. Others just try not to get stepped on. This is also true of small dogs, which tend to be either world-class barkers or world-class slinkers.

I do it all. I dress big, I bark, and I slink.

I *escabullirse*d into American Lit class and took my usual seat near the windows a few seconds before the 7:40 chime. A few minutes later, the kid with the BMW walked in. Mr. Clemens gave him a raised-eyebrow look.

"Sorry I'm late, sir," he said. "My name is Shayne. With a *Y*. Shayne Blank. I just transferred here."

Mr. Clemens, startled by all his politeness, directed Shayne-with-a-*Y* Blank to the empty desk next to me.

Here's what was weird. Every one of us had our eyes on him, the way we would stare at any new face, but this kid appeared to be perfectly comfortable, relaxed, confident, and alert. I've met cats that could pull that off—that combination of hyperalertness and megaconfidence— but I'd never seen it in a human. So, after class, being a friendly and inquisitive type of guy, I followed him into the hall and introduced myself properly. We went through the whole where-are-you-from-what-are-you-doing-here routine—he told me he was originally from Fartlick, Idaho, and that his dad was on a secret mission to Afghanistan, and that his mom was in the Witness Protection Program, and he was living with his aunt.

"I suppose she's an astronaut or something," I said.

"Yes. But from another planet."

I liked his sense of humor.

"I thought maybe you were from the South. Because of your accent."

"I have no accent," he said, in an accent.

"So is Blank your real name? Or an alias?"

He frowned. "You don't like it?"

I was opening my mouth to say something back to him when I felt a hand clamp down on my shoulder.

"Hey, Mikey."

"Hey, Jon," I said, trying to act as if I was glad to see him.

Jon Brande was borderline movie star handsome, with blond hair, sparkly blue eyes, a strong chin, and a toothpaste-ad smile—the picture of a vibrant, healthy teenager, ready to graduate with honors, accept a basketball scholarship to a Big Ten university, and go on to enjoy a brilliant career in politics. Except that Jon had been kicked off the basketball team his sophomore year and his grades were just barely passing.

Also, he was a violent, psychotic, drug-dealing creep.

"Listen." He hung his arm around my shoulders and turned me so our backs were to Shayne. "You got room for this in your backpack?" He handed me a brown paper lunch bag. It was limp and wrinkled, as if it had been opened and closed several times. "Just hold it for me. I'll get it back from you after school."

All my alarm bells were going off, but there was no way I could refuse. Jon was big, he was a senior, and he scared the crap out of me. I took the bag. I didn't have to ask him what was in it, but I couldn't help asking, "Why?"

"No reason." He winked and walked off.

Believe me, it is very creepy to get winked at by Jon Brande.

Shayne said, "Friend of yours?"

"Not really." I stuffed the paper bag into my backpack. "He's my sister's boyfriend."

PETE HAUTMAN

Transcending stories of life-changing friendship from Benjamin Alire Sáenz